BLEEDING HEARTS

A DECLAN ROSEWOOD MYSTERY

ERIN LARK MAPLES

LODESTAR LITERARY

For Jacque
Who makes everything fun

ONE

Declan—who'd yet to get used to the name—fanned a stack of twenties in front of his face. Their wrinkled edges, taped tears, and minute details created a faded peacock tail. He marveled at the filthy paper assigned arbitrary values by humans. *Fascinating.*

The man behind the counter pushed a yellow receipt toward Declan. "Mr. Rosewood? You'll need this for pick-up."

Declan spared a glance at the paper, scrawled words straying outside gray lines. He looked at the man whose presence he sought to forget. Yellowing teeth, absent chin, and two-day beard gave him the look of a tired beaver. Lank, greasy hair parted in the middle, curled behind too-long ears, and streaked back toward a squat neck. People came in such variety, he marveled. He leaned over the paper to read. "Pick-up?"

"You've got thirty days to return with the money," the man said, shifting a wad of something across his lower jaw with his tongue. His lip bulged, and a spot of drool gathered at the corner of his mouth. A too-tight *Biker Babes* T-shirt stretched over his belly and fluttered above a pair of plaid pajama pants. A rack of weapons made a stark backdrop, their potential behind glass, lock, and key. "If not, it's mine."

Declan squinted at the man. Were these words a sign from above? He'd just parted with the third-from-the-last of his most precious belongings from his former life to this creature, a sacrifice of the highest order. Declan spared a last glance at the lute, its gilded curls flashing against the honeyed wood. He'd had many a night with that rounded back in his lap, the strings taut beneath his fingertips, not unlike his midsummer lovers. But that was before.

Before. To have a time that came ahead of this moment, there had to be an after. His after was the focus. He may return for this instrument of his past life—or he may not. Lutes would come and go, but freedom was priceless.

Declan laid the crisp receipt alongside his stack of cash, folded and pocketed the wad—pockets were a delight—and headed into the misty morning.

On the sidewalk, he quick-stepped around a flock of pigeons cooing over scattered bread crumbs. "Pardon me, noble steeds. Give Mother my love." Declan paused in his step, looked around, then crouched down to address the birds. "On second thought, friends, better keep quiet, eh?" The birds continued to scavenge which Declan took as a sign of agreement.

Declan crossed at the corner. The street ahead pitched upward, past an old building the color of melted butter. It was a severe structure, ringed in white detail like a bygone wedding cake. Declan had yet to behold such a confection in person— he avoided the drama of weddings, especially now—but he'd seen pictures. Two lovers swearing to love each other and let none come between. A little family drama and that notion of marriage went right out the window for Declan. Forever was easy to promise to those with a brief lifeline and a lack of meddlesome relatives.

Declan paused in front of a large sign anchored in the brief front lawn. "Historical Museum..." he mused aloud. "Wonder if they have any of my family in there."

"Are your people local, dear?"

The voice startled Declan. He turned to find a short woman with frizzy gray hair watching him with beady brown eyes. She'd popped out from behind the sign like a piece of unexpected toast.

Toast. This was on his *First Day* list. In preparation for his new diet, his sister made him memorize a handful of local takeout menus, so he'd understand what to eat. Avocado toast was a repeat on several leaflets. The cash in his pocket pressed against Declan's thigh. *Grocery money.*

"...nigh everyone has cannery in their blood around here. My father, his father, and his before him. It was a proud tradition in the Thatcher family. Who were your people?"

Declan stared at the woman. She yammered with the tenacity of a house sparrow. More than a head shorter than Declan, silvered curls framed a round face. Wrinkles betrayed a life of sun and time. A pair of reading glasses dipped in the collar of her blouse. Zipped into a bright red raincoat, she wielded a trowel in one hand, purple gardening gloves speckled with soil. She blinked, waiting. He rejoined the discussion.

"Oh. I'm not from here. I...uh...didn't know anyone was listening." Declan gave the little chuckle learned from watching what his sister called *reality television*. He'd marveled at the self-deprecating cues people used to apologize for themselves or signal other intentions.

"I should think someone like you would be used to an audience," she said, eyeing him from top to bottom and back.

Declan stilled. *Here it comes.* Throughout history, he'd bathed in attention. Craved it. Now, it was old news—a nuisance, even. When he'd asked his perpetually gloomy mother to give him a more familiar appearance to match his new surroundings, she'd scoffed, suggesting that he might as well cut her heart out on his way to the coast.

Golden boy, it was.

"It's only that you're a bit...bright. Wouldn't you say?"

The glasses. While his details may be fuzzy, whatever her prescription, he would stand out. Declan looked down at his neon yellow track suit. His mother insisted he wear the monstrosity so as not to be hit by a car on day one. He'd balked, she'd insisted. In her mind, Astoria was a godless, violent bedlam on the edges of the continent instead of a sleepy town slouched against a hill. *Note to self, change as soon as possible.*

Declan cleared his throat. "It was a gift."

"I see," the woman said, her pinched expression unpacking who would gift–let alone treasure–such a present. "So then, you're new here?"

"Yes," Declan said, grateful for the change of subject. "Just arrived. On my way to..." He consulted his phone, a plastic device his sister assured him was a necessity. "Irving and 16th." He pointed up the incline, proud of his new navigational skill set.

"That so?" the woman said, eyeing him. She patted at her jacket pockets and then the top of her head for the glasses, as though to examine his screen herself.

"Lovely chat," he said, before he fell under her scrutiny. "See you around?" Declan strode off before she could get a closer look.

Three blocks up, and he gasped for breath. His hamstrings and buttocks burned from the exertion. Declan tuned into this new form he wore, its strengths and limits a continuous curiosity. His earthbound muscles struggled with stamina, aching for a rest. He would have to put them to a test, learn what humans did to maintain gladiator status.

At number 1608, Declan faced an iron arch. Two dozen brick steps curved upward to meet a wide front porch, and a short hedge edged the yard. White, peeling siding striped the house, garage, and a shed, moss sneaking in at the eaves. Three stories teetered upward from ground level. A slate gray roof formed a hat for the structures. In a small window set in the top story, a curtain fluttered.

Declan took a deep breath and unlatched the gate. It creaked in response, clattering shut behind him with finality. He bounded up the steps to the porch and knocked. Next to the door was a mailbox affixed to the wall at an angle and a wide porch swing.

The door opened into a wave of Pavarotti and baked goods. A woman with blond hair braided and wrapped across her crown in a halo wore an apron emblazoned with *On a Roll*. Flour dusted its navy front and her pink cheeks.

"Hello," she said, her throaty voice betraying the source of the flush.

"I'm Declan," he said, and rearranged his mouth into a smile that was big but not creepy. He'd spent hours in front of a mirror practicing his expressions. "Declan Rosewood."

"Ah," she said, still staring. Thick lashes blinked over soft gray eyes.

"Here for the room?"

"Oh. Yes. I mean. Oh, my. Uh..." She broke eye contact and backed into the house, making way for Declan and his backpack. "Can I help you carry anything?"

"No need. I travel light." He followed her inside as she untied the apron from her waist, removed it, and flung the garment over a kitchen stool. Cinnamon and cardamom perfumed the air. She grabbed a lemon-shaped timer from the counter, twisted it, then clutched the ticking device as though it were a life preserver.

Unsure of where to go, Declan idled in the cheery living

room. An overstuffed couch bursting with pillows crowded one corner of the room, a ghastly floral painting hanging above its bulk. A piano anchored a second corner, its bench waiting for a player. Atop the instrument sat a small, round speaker out of which music poured into the ground floor of the massive house. The final bar of "Recondita Armonia" washed over him.

"Jessica." The woman offered her hand. "If we can start over." She avoided his eyes, staring at a spot just over his ear. "Call me Jess, though. Everyone does."

"Declan," he said, and looked down at her open palm. *Just try,* he thought, and shook her hand. Warmth spread between them, a faint vibration palpable between their skin. There was a shock of electricity and a spark in the air.

Jess yanked her hand back in reflex. "I...I...uh...must have been the static." Jess licked her lips and met his gaze.

Uh oh. "Must have been." Declan faked a need to scratch the back of his neck.

Jess recovered, giving her head a brief shake. "Thank you for paying so far ahead, sight unseen."

Declan nodded. His mother's other parting gift—rent paid for the year. "Er...my sister picked it out. Your description was more than adequate."

"I'll give you a tour of my room. I mean, of the *house*," Jess said. She avoided his gaze and brushed past him into the living room. "She's an older gal, but she's steadfast. Original wallpaper in several rooms, same with the furniture and windows. They give great night...I mean, light."

Declan peered at the woman. Ripples of heat, sweaty palms. A quickened pulse at her throat. His new life would be complicated. *Thanks, Mom.* Following behind Jess, he rolled his eyes heavenward, in case his mother were watching. He broached the awkwardness with Jess. "Are you a fan of opera?"

"My grandmother taught me to love it," she said. "This

was her house. My mother would bring me to visit each Sunday. We'd make a batch of cookies and curl up with a record of the greats as the rain pattered against the window-panes. I have her to thank for so many of my passions—music and baking are just two of them. In a way, I like to think she's still here with me." Her voice wavered as she regarded the worn wallpaper and furnishings. "The music takes me back, you know?"

"You loved her," Declan said, a simple declaration. With all the uncertainty of his new life, the ability to understand the heart hadn't wavered.

"Her and this house. It's been in our family for ages. Feels like a family member at this point." Jessica blinked back tears. "Forgive me," she said. "It's been a week. I'm not usually so… emotional." With the back of her thumb, she wiped at her eyes and took a deep breath. "At any rate, it's just me rattling around in here now. Renting out the apartment helps. It gets lonely, you know?"

Declan studied her. He'd seen the gamut of what love and loss did to a person. Recently, he'd felt something close to this, himself. "It's a magnificent house, a treasure. I hope I won't be in your way."

"Not possible," Jessica said, laughing through her tears. "There's a separate entrance so you can come and go whenever you want. All night if you like." Jess's cheeks reddened again. "You know, if you need to borrow the oven or something. Here, I'll show you."

Jess snagged a key off the counter and handed it to Declan. He followed her out the back door. "Do you have a car?"

Declan shook his head. Learning public transport was a new—but intriguing—task on his to-do list. "I planned to walk, mostly. Should be a pleasant change."

"Good for the glutes," Jess said, then grimaced. The lemon timer dinged in her hand. She gestured to a set of stairs attached to the side of a small, two-story garage anchoring the side yard. "Head on up. Have a look around and then let me know what you think." She hurried into the house.

Declan was alone in the yard. He assessed the rickety stairs, then climbed. The steps creaked beneath his feet, wood complaining under his weight. At the top, the key fit the lock, and he was inside.

The hush of the apartment soothed him. A place of his own. Tidy and freshly painted, the space was clean and welcoming. Jessica's post offered a furnished studio with a view—and didn't disappoint.

Declan toured the remainder of his space. The tiny bathroom revealed a giant shower head sticking out above a plastic curtain covered with a map of the world. In the main space, a big bed covered in a navy duvet stood against one wall, a pile of seashell-decorated pillows awaiting his slumber. In front of him, a small kitchen gave way to a brief living area. Two captain's chairs bracketed a coffee table in front of a large picture window. On the back wall hung a painting of a massive sailing ship out at sea. Small, convenient, and all his.

Perfection.

Declan dropped his backpack on the bed and took in his view. This side faced the hill. Rows of houses marched upward like ants. The leaves of the neighbor's oak tree brushed the glass.

A misty rain smattered the window with droplets. He remembered the woman in her red slicker, his embarrassment over his clothing. Five minutes later, he wore a pair of jeans, a black sweater, and sneakers. *Dowdy professor,* his sister had tutted as she watched him pack. He was comfortable, though, and camouflaged.

Outside, he debated the back door, uncertain, then rounded the house to the front. The door yawned open, and Declan went in.

Jessica flapped a dishcloth over several pans of rolls, a phone wedged between her ear and shoulder. "That's not going to happen...I know you mean well, but...You aren't listening to me. This is exactly what I—" Jessica froze, catching sight of Declan. "I've got to go," she said into the speaker, and hung up.

"Sorry, I didn't mean to interrupt you," Declan said.

"You didn't," Jessica said. "An ex. Wants to get back together. Says he loves me, wants me to move in with him, but...it's complicated."

"Is that what you want?" This was Declan's territory. His bread and butter. He could leave the work behind, but the instinctual pull ate at him no matter how far he roamed.

Jessica shook her head. "I did, once. Then things started taking off for my business and we both got busy. But a part of me...still thinks yes. It's why I take his calls. Is that crazy?"

Declan shook his head. "Not crazy." He ate this up, a genuine opportunity to interact. "What do you want from a relationship?"

"I don't know. Maybe someone who will be around, not always chasing after the next shiny thing that comes along. Someone satisfied with the simple things in life. The sound of rain on the roof, the taste of a Sunday roast. I'd like a guy who'll support my dreams, for once."

"Then say no to anything that's not that," Declan said. So many people knew what they needed but allowed others to sabotage them at every turn. It takes conviction, a little bravery, and faith to get what you want.

"Thanks," Jess said. "I'm getting back out there. Got a date next week, so we'll see. Anyway, enough about me." She tossed the dish towel on the counter. With a pair of tongs, she hefted a roll onto a plate and slathered it in cream cheese frosting. She handed him the plate. "A few burned," she said, "but I salvaged most of them. Let me know what you think. Everything look all right in the apartment?"

The smell of the roll was intoxicating. Declan wanted to bury his face in its pillowy, cinnamon spiral. "Absolutely." He took a big bite and moaned. Icing dripped down the side of his hand and wrapped around his wrist. "This is...wow."

"Almost perfect." Her brow furrowed, arms crossed.

"Almost? They're a...revelation."

"Thanks," she said, and the blush was back. "I've got a brunch on the calendar in just a few weeks. Have to taste test the recipes. Tweak what I can while I have a chance. I'm debating using lavender in the dough. Or maybe rose petals on top? As Grandma told me, every recipe's an interview."

"You're a caterer? That's incredible."

Jess shrugged. "Trying to be. I do birthday cakes all the time, baby showers, things like that. But I'd like to branch out. I have a professional kitchen in town," she said. "Have to use it for events, of course. But I start off here, with family recipes."

Declan gorged himself on the roll, its unraveling swirl dripping with glaze. He licked at his fingers, not wanting to miss a drop. This was what he'd been missing, the messiness of life. "Guessing you're booked up with clients."

"Getting there—but it's stressful. I'm saving up for my own restaurant. In the meantime, I'm pitching to a councilman's bride next week. I'd kill to get that job—two hundred people and four courses."

"They'd be fools not to hire you," Declan said, eyeing his last bite of roll. "There aren't words for how sinful this tastes."

Jessica bit her lip. "Thank you. And hey, you're a florist, right? Maybe you could do the flowers?"

Declan froze. He was so focused on the heaven in his mouth he'd all but forgotten his persona. Recovering, he stepped to the sink to wash his hands, aware of Jess's gaze following him. "I'm more of a houseplants guy, but I appreciate the tip," he said. When he turned around, Jess held out a dish towel. Declan was careful not to touch her fingers. "Speaking of work, I'm picking up my keys today. Better get down there and see what's what."

Jessica lifted her eyes to meet his. "Don't be a stranger," she said, the corner of her mouth curling upward. "Gets pretty lonely rattling around in here by myself."

"I'll remember that," Declan said, and gave her a warm smile. Jess was kind. He'd have to keep his boundaries, but that was nothing new.

Declan was half out the front door when Jess called, "Which space did you rent?"

"Oh, it's 1214 Commercial," Declan said. "Do you know it?" He wondered if she'd follow him. This happened sometimes, especially with the lovelorn. Couldn't help themselves.

"Great spot," Jess said. "The old Ram & Rose."

Declan frowned. "Ram and—?" *Harmonia!*

Two

Declan fumed for the entirety of his walk back down the hill toward the busy streets near the water. Astoria's business district spread out in a straightforward grid—if a little wiggly on the edges. At each street corner he'd shake his head in frustration, then storm off toward his destination, pedestrians peering after him in the wake of his irritation.

On Commercial, he spotted a purple and orange-fronted yoga studio, a pink lotus centered on its sign. Next door, as promised by the rental agreement, was another retail space, similarly sized and empty. The place was dim within, space receding into blackness behind the front window.

Declan glanced up at the shop's sign. *Ram & Rose, Est. 1813.* "Not funny!" Declan pursed his lips, unsure if his sister could hear, let alone see, his consternation.

"Might be," said a woman by his side. "Could be you who doesn't get the joke."

Declan whirled to find a short, older woman with spiky electric pink hair parked at his elbow. Like Declan, she faced the shop, her arms crossed. She wore a pair of black and purple cheetah-print leggings and a shirt that said *Heavily Meditated.*

"By the feet of Laverna, what is it with people sneaking up on me?"

The corner of the woman's mouth turned up. "No harm intended. I come in peace—with keys." She jangled a set in front of him before clasping it back within her palm. "I take it you're the new guy?"

Declan studied the woman. There was something familiar about her, something ancient. It wasn't the gray at her temples, nor the wrinkles that creased her brow. It was in the tone of her voice—something round, hollow, and echoing. He willed his overstuffed memory to sort out her identity. *Like searching for a needle in a haystack,* he thought, never having seen an actual haystack. "Declan Rosewood," he said, still looking at her. "Do I...know you?"

"I'm Maeve. That's me over there," she said, and turned her face from his scrutiny to point at the brightly painted shopfront. "*Mudra* is my studio." She made a quick set of gestures with her fingers. "You know—yoga?"

"Ah, I see," Declan said, but didn't. This woman mystified him. It was as though a bell rang in the far-off shelving within the library of his eons-old brain, but he couldn't reach back that far. "Forgive me. You seem...familiar."

The sprite of a septuagenarian put her hands on her hips. "Happens all the time. You'll see. The longer you work down here, the more people will claim to know you. It'll get to where you even recognize the tourists."

Exhaustion pressed at Declan's temples. "So, those are my keys?"

Maeve smiled. "Class doesn't start for a half hour. Let me give you the tour." Without waiting for Declan, Maeve wrestled a key into the lock. With a creak, the door swung open in two halves. "You can latch those together," she said, and held both parts of the door open.

"Why would a door split in half?" Declan said.

"Crowd control." Maeve ushered him in and let the lower half swing shut. It latched with a firm click. "Or maybe to get a little air in here. Whew, that's rank."

Declan's eyes adjusted to the dim in a flicker of blinks before the scent hit him. Something dank and skunk-like permeated the walls. "What *is* that?"

"Your neighbors," Maeve said, and chuckled. "Don't worry, they're quiet and the security on this block can't be beat. Might want to get your vents checked, though. It's an old building."

Declan nodded. "Vents, got it." He ran a visual check of the space, taking mental note of what would need polishing—or a trip to the dumpster.

Peeling handbills covered the walls, bright blue print against faded yellow paper. Layers of band posters and comedy nights papered the walls. A giant beverage cooler loomed against one wall, unplugged. An old-fashioned cash register anchored the behemoth of a bar that occupied the bulk of the front section. Two torn-apart booths were all that remained of the seating, vinyl peeling from their surfaces. On one side of the brief hallway was a door marked *Loo*, and on the other side, a swinging door suggested a kitchen. A stack of flattened cardboard boxes lay in a heap on the black-and-white tiles. *Vintage*, Declan thought. Dust was a thick blanket.

"Was quite the place in its day. Many scandalous activities took place between these walls. Bootlegging, gambling, and the like. But that was decades ago, according to folk who were here back then."

"You weren't?" Declan fished for clues about the woman. Memories—or legends—tugged at the recesses of his mind.

Maeve lifted an eyebrow at him. "No, I wasn't. Not a

local. Been here a handful of years, but I love it. You will, too. The place grows on you, like a barnacle."

Declan drifted around the shop, running a finger through a line of dust and picking up an old, stained menu. He turned a slow circle, taking in the leaking ceiling tiles, the sink full of broken glass, and the massive mirrored wall behind the bar. He'd known this life wouldn't be easy, and if he couldn't make it through a little manual labor, he wouldn't last the year. "It'll do," he said, "just fine."

"Then I'll leave you to it. Anything comes up—I'm next door. Unless the sign is flipped to *Closed*. I don't answer knocks mid-sutra."

"Got it," Declan said, noting the slew of new words he'd need to look up. His list of vocabulary grew by the minute. He made a mental note to get his own door sign.

"You should come to a class sometime. First one's on me. Schedule's posted out front," Maeve said, letting herself out the front door. "It'll do you some good. Those who are all bulked up are some of the worst at staying limber."

Declan stepped to the half-open door and leaned out to call after her. "What do you mean by that?" But she was gone. "For someone deep into their crone years, that one's fast on her feet."

A rush of kids on skateboards whooshed by, and Declan jumped back, the wheels inches from his toes. One kid skidded in a half-turn, his wheels grinding against the concrete. He pressed down on the end of his board with a foot, catching the top end with his hand. "You gotta be careful, mister. Can't be popping out like that. You'll take a crit."

The boy swam in giant black jeans, their cuffs ragged. He wore a *Ramones* T-shirt and a belt with a giant, smiley-faced buckle. His hair was shaggy, lank in the misty rain. He brushed it back off his eyes with one hand, the limp brown locks falling right back into place.

"A what?"

"Crit. A cri-ti-cal hit. You know—" The boy smashed his palms together in a violent collision.

Declan blinked. "Oh. I didn't know this was a war zone." He frowned and cased the sidewalk. "I thought I was safe."

The kid grinned. "Is anywhere really safe?"

"Guess not." In all his preparation, Declan hadn't studied teenagers. In his line of work, they were largely ignored, too rash for the finer details, too flighty for deep investment. Now, however, Declan marveled at the boy's bravery, his charm, and his knowledge of the battlefield. He could have been anywhere between twelve and fifteen, by Declan's unpracticed eye, but wiser than his years. "I'm Declan. I'm new."

"Pax," the boy said. "What'll it be?"

"What?" Declan was wholly unprepared for this conversation.

Pax pointed up to the old sign above the shop. "This."

Declan followed his gaze. "Oh. Of course. A plant shop."

"Sounds boring," the kid said, and shrugged. "See ya." He dropped his board and was off.

Dust covered Declan's clothes, evidence of his afternoon in the shop. He'd hauled the boxes to a dumpster, cleaned the glass out of the sink, and swept the space with a derelict broom he'd found in the otherwise sparse kitchen. The broom rested on half its original bristles, leaning against a crusted silver machine labeled *Lil-Os*. Declan washed up at the sink, running a gritty bar of green soap over his hands. Given all the new experiences in his human form, he found washing up to be one of his favorites. Jess would know where he could find towels like hers and a bottle of the lemony soap he'd used at her sink. He pocketed his supply list and locked the double door behind him. The keys had a pleasant weight to them, a promise of more days to come.

Back on Irving, Declan bypassed the house and headed for his own steps. He'd stopped at a taco truck to pick up dinner —a mammoth burrito entitled "The California"—and looked forward to this culinary experiment.

"Have a sec?" Jess leaned out the back door. Her hair was knotted at the back of her neck, twisted into a clip. A fresh slick of gloss shone on her lips. She had the look of an old film actress, ready for a cameo. "I'd like to show you something."

Oh no. Here it comes.

When he'd made the arrangements to come here, to give up his life in search of something different, he'd wanted to leave his past life behind—all of it. But when he'd shed the past in search of a new self, his mother's vanity maintained the one thing he loathed most. He was going to have to let this nice, sweet woman down easily—then pray he wouldn't need to house hunt.

Declan set the bag on the steps. "You and I have a date with destiny," he said to the burrito, then crossed the yard.

"Won't take long," Jess said on his approach. She beckoned him inside. "It's worth it, I promise."

Inside, Jess was already halfway up the flight of stairs leading to the second story. "Uh..." He paused at the bottom of the steps. Declan was going to have to be clear. "I don't think I...that you..."

Jess paused at the halfpace. "You aren't afraid of heights or anything, are you?"

Declan checked himself. What was she getting at—a rendezvous on the roof? "Definitely not."

"Follow me," she said, and disappeared from sight.

Declan climbed the steps, puffing out his cheeks with breath. Yet again, he would have to break the heart of some obsessed human. *No, I won't bed you. Please don't touch me like that. I am flattered, but not available. No, I don't need someone to "take care" of me. Please put your clothes on.*

Prepared, he crested the landing. But Jess was gone. At the end of the hallway, a ladder led up through an opening in the ceiling. Vestiges of daylight fell through the gap. Declan climbed upward, one rung at a time.

"Come on up," Jess said when she spotted Declan's head at the top of the ladder. Jess stood in a tiny vestibule at the top of the house. Not large enough for a room, it was an attic of sorts. She stuck a leg out of a large casement window, opened to the growing dusk, and hoisted herself outside.

When Declan copied her move, he found himself on a short platform that surrounded the topmost story of the old house. There was a flimsy railing, curly cues of metal decorating its length. "It's the widow's walk," she explained, as though he'd understand.

Declan leaned to peer over the edge. "It's high up," he said, a momentary blossom of fear in his guts.

"I love it up here," Jess said. She turned her smile toward the setting sun as Declan inched his way out to her.

The view was spectacular. They could see in every direction across the small city, its lights winking on. There were the old cannery buildings, the tower on the hillside, the barges waiting in the water. To the west, where the Columbia emptied itself into the ocean, the sun dove for the horizon, a rippling orange ball shading the sky in ribbons of pink and violet.

"Stunning." Declan's eyes filled with the bright, waning light.

"To be fair, it isn't always like this. But when it is, it's..."

"Heaven." Declan wrapped his hands around the rail, the metal warming under his touch. "And here we are, perched like birds above it all."

"Whenever things seem a little too heavy, I come up here.

Somehow, feeling like a small part of all this—" she gestured outward over the streets of houses, the bricked downtown with its massive white Astor building, cars motoring down the streets—"reminds me that no matter what, there's so much out there. So many wonderful things ahead of me."

Declan watched her as the setting sun caressed her jaw in shades of gold. Her hair, flecked with copper, escaped from underneath a bandana. Amber eyes lit up with the possibility of the moment. To look at this world with raw wonder must be glorious. "Stunning," he said, his voice a whisper in the wind.

"Well. That's pretty much it," she said with a laugh, as the burning ball of light dipped beneath the horizon. "Until tomorrow, that is."

"Thanks for showing me," he said, his smile pure and unaltered. This was new; he could find a woman beautiful and leave things at that. Whatever she thought of him, they could enjoy each other's company as is.

"Happy to share," Jess said. She beamed at him, Venus winking in the sky behind her. "But watch out for that first step down."

THREE

Tuesday struck with promise. Declan awoke in his own apartment daydreaming of the day ahead. This was all new, and intoxicating. He donned a pair of dark sunglasses and set foot into the morning.

Astoria. Declan consulted the brochure Harmonia had tucked inside a guidebook she'd packed alongside a pair of rainboots, a box of granola bars (Declan had two of these for breakfast) and something called a can opener. He unfolded the length of the glossy paper to scan the map printed on one side. Named after John Jacob Astor—before changing to Fort George, then back again—the city was the oldest established on the west coast, its location chosen carefully by planners who could only dream of what it would become.

Declan took in the looming bridge that spilled into a downtown that was half industry, half multi-colored residences and tried to picture how it must have grown over the centuries. Fur trappers of yesteryear gave way to a maritime museum. Stark bricked mansions of the wealthy dotted a hillside covered in cottages and bungalows. Horse-drawn carriages became electric cars. Sea lions called out from underneath the docks, and cormorants stretched their wings toward what little sunlight peeked through the clouds. Today's version of the city bustled with comings and goings of people, cars, and ships. No longer a fort, Astoria still held court as an anchor of activity.

The location was perfect. To prove that he was more than a one-trick caricature, he'd needed somewhere to try out an ordinary human life. Astoria, with its tumultuous history, turncoat weather, and the formidable mouth of a mighty river, would suit his purpose. He'd boasted that such a place would be a true test of his abilities to endure without the trappings of power. Here was a chance to prove he was more than the Olympic pretty boy, drowning in privilege and caught up in every lovers' spat. For what hardships would lie on the warm sands of a Mediterranean coast? The forests of the Amazon? Declan had something to prove, and he wasn't cutting corners.

As he walked, Declan took in the morning sights of everyday Astoria. At a scrap of a park, he watched a woman play fetch with a standard poodle. She'd dressed the charcoal-colored dog in a bright yellow raincoat, her own jacket a matching shade. Nearby, a man bundled up in a wool coat and scarf, occupied a bench facing the water. He cradled a hefty book in his lap, dragging a finger across the page as he read.

Declan ventured onto the boardwalk, passing an Italian restaurant, an ice cream shop, a place that sold stained glass, and a jeweler that specialized in pearls. The last was odd as Pacific oysters didn't produce jewelry-pearls according to the guidebook, but who was a shopkeeper to get between a customer and their purchase? Declan added this to his growing list of peculiarities of human beings. Would he, too, start craving beachy knick knacks despite the lack of beach? Bemoan the difference between a mist and a drizzle while shifting his wardrobe from business casual to thick, cabled sweaters and corduroy pants?

He could hear Harmonia's peals of laughter at such a trans-formation. She'd done her best to help him assimilate before the journey. They'd watched movies she dubbed classics, like *Die Hard* and *The Princess Bride.* Then there was reality television—which Declan decried as little more than humans yelling at each other for forty-five minutes in semi-exotic locations. When he'd asked for books, she'd plunked down her collection of romance novels. Most had women in diaphanous silks clinging to broad-chested men with flowing hair. Tight on time, he made do.

Declan knew that not all men are six-foot tall, muscular lumberjacks named Erick or Slade and that the women weren't in a constant state of half-dress, presenting heaving cleavage for inspection, and that the average adult didn't have secret babies and super rich families. Most people were a less than glamorous average, thus his former day job. Humans, the real ones, required adjusted expectations.

Still, living among them for a year would bring its own wisdom. That's why he was here, after all. Declan decided he would say yes to the opportunities—whatever they may be—and see where that took him.

The first was an incredible smell, like a roasted, nutty caramel, wafting outward from a small shop on the pier. *Coffee.*

Pastry House was spray painted across the large store window. Inside, shiplap covered the walls. Several small red tables huddled together, a few diners parked in the matching chairs. A pastry case commanded the front counter, a massive espresso machine to one side. Behind, a doorway led into a kitchen gleaming with stainless steel.

A stout woman occupied the place behind the counter. With long-handled tongs, she shifted several stacks of croissants to make room for others. Moon-shaped hand pies joined Danishes, cookies, and cinnamon rolls jostling for space on the shelves. Declan unwrapped his scarf from around his neck and removed his sunglasses to get a better look. As customers finished their orders, he made his way to the front of the line and beamed at her. She let out the slightest gasp and froze in place.

Declan once asked a former paramour to describe his looks while they lounged atop a tangle of sheets. A human woman —a textile artist—she'd regarded him, thoughtful. A wrinkle appeared over one brow as she drew her gaze along his length and back up to his face. "You are," she'd said, "what sculptors can never capture. For how could they match the bronze of your skin, those golden eyes, and the light you've swallowed whole?"

In front of him now, in this windswept, watery town, stood a woman wielding tongs, the purveyor of coffee and breakfast. Declan heard murmurs from those behind him in line, irritated by the unseen delay. Confronted by this mute barista with heavenly buns, Declan determined to smooth over this transaction. He'd order his goodies to go, making as quick a stop as possible.

"Good morning," he said, mentally cranking his mirror-coached grin down a few notches to a pleasant smile.

"Um. Hello," the woman said, her husky voice spurred to respond. Crow's feet framed her eyes, and her hair was a bottled brown, yet the hint of an accent and a wall of photographs from exotic places suggested an adventurer. "How can I serve you? I mean, what would you like?"

"Smells great in here. How about a croissant and a—"

Zzzuzzz. Zuzzz. Bang! Sounds from the adjacent wall cut off Declan's order. A customer dropped his mug which clattered into its saucer.

The woman huffed at the interruption, glaring at the wall. "Not again!"

Declan looked from the woman to the wall and back. "If now isn't a good time, I can come back?"

"No, no, please stay." The woman held up a hand to Declan. "It's only my neighbor. She insists on having workers in and out while my customers are trying to enjoy themselves. I'd give anything for it to stop."

Clang. Rattle. Zzzzuzz. The flush on the woman's face betrayed her continued frustration and embarrassment.

"In that case, I'll take the croissant and a vanilla latte"

The woman nodded and turned to the machine, the hiss of the device battling with the construction sounds next door. Declan perused posters on the wall advertising massage therapists, a tarot reader, and a community night at Mudra. He debated Maeve's invitation. His sister's books hadn't described yoga classes, and the reality television contestants only talked about wanting to do yoga. He'd need to investigate.

"One vanilla latte and a croissant—on the house."

Declan protested. "You don't have to do that—" A handful of his new bills were crammed into his crisp wallet.

"So you'll come back," she said.

"I'll do that, thank you." Declan pressed some cash into the tip jar, collected his order, and headed back into the waning sunshine.

Croissant in one hand, coffee in the other, Declan paused outside the next storefront to take a bite. Flakes of pastry crumbled to the ground where a flock of pigeons took on cleanup duty. "Hello again, fellas." When he took a sip of the steaming beverage, he glanced into the wide window of the neighboring shop. Sure enough, there was a worker in coveralls, drill in hand. He spoke to someone digging into a large cardboard box. The pile of hair atop their head was familiar.

Jessica.

Declan knocked on the glass. Both people looked up. The man frowned, but a wide grin spread across Jessica's face. She pulled open the door and ushered him inside.

"Check it out," she said. "I've got new shelves!"

On one wall, a set of wire racks held a collection of cookware. Jessica had unpacked a standing mixer, a stack of baking sheets, and two giant bowls. "Looks great," Declan said. "This is your place?"

Jessica nodded. "It's tiny, but it works for now. Got the rent cheap, too, since there wasn't much here to begin with."

All but the front few feet of the angled space was the kitchen. On either side of the front door, shelving held disposable pans, aluminum foil, and a box of business cards emblazoned with *Catering by Jess.* She'd used every inch of the space, efficiency at every turn.

"I think I could use your advice in setting up my shop. I'd like to keep some of the funky fixtures and the bar, but I've got to figure out where to put everything else."

"I'd be happy to help! I've got about a million macarons to make for a church tea, but other than that, I've got some open afternoons."

"Perfect. Come by anytime. I'm giving the place a fresh coat of paint today. Speaking of paint, I'm headed to a place called—"Declan checked his phone—"Burt's Hardware."

"Up two blocks and down three," Jess said. Her curls brushed back from her face when she turned her head to point out the window.

"Uh, I think you might be missing an earring," Declan said.

Jess patted at the sides of her face, her cheeks flushed. "Oh," she said, patting both ears. Only one gold hoop remained. She unhooked it from her ear and slid it into her pocket. "Let's hope it's not in a cake!" Declan laughed and she nodded at his cup. "So, you've been next door?"

"I have," Declan said. He wouldn't get involved in any kind of rivalry, but this was his landlord. Lying about the buttery, melt-in-his-mouth pastry he'd devoured would be obvious. "Tasty place."

"Sofia has incredible talent. Not my biggest fan, though," Jess said. "At least not recently. But I've picked up a few tips from her over the years."

Declan caught a hint of sadness in her voice. "Well, I look forward to tasting your experiments—if you need a guinea pig."

Jess laughed, the gap in her front teeth on full display. "Might take advantage of that!"

"I'm a willing participant," he said. Jess was charming, and if he hadn't sworn off dalliances...well. He would enjoy having her in proximity, nonetheless.

"One sec," she said. "While you're here, how about weighing in on that wedding?"

After discussing her proposed menu at length and accepting the takeaway box she handed him, Declan waved to Jess and headed out into the fresh air. The clouds slunk overhead, promising rain. He picked up his pace. Gulls glided between rooftops, calling to each other. At the hardware store, Declan ticked off the bulk of his list and made a beeline for his shop. A heavy mist descended as he unlocked the front door.

A short stack of mail waited inside on the floor, no doubt shoved through the built-in brass slot in the door. Declan heaved two cans of black paint onto the bar top and stooped to pick up the pile of envelopes. A few bills, an advertisement for new windows, and a postcard from his mom. There was no stamp, but there didn't need to be.

Declan stepped to the window, glancing up and down the street, but he knew she wouldn't be there. The card he held had a picture of a ram, a rose behind one horn. "Hilarious." He flipped over the card to read her note.

My Darling,

Things here aren't the same without you. Your brothers have only each other with whom to do battle. Harmonia does her best, but even she tires of the constant bickering. Your father is off on some new campaign. You know what they say —the more things change, the more they stay the same. I'm proud of your new adventure, even though it hurts. Miss you something fierce.

All my love, Mom

Declan pressed the card to his chest. For the first time, he knew what it was to be homesick.

Four

They arrived in boxes of all shapes and sizes, carried in by a uniform-clad delivery driver who winked at Declan. Many of the packages contained plants wrapped in a tissue-like material, others had their pots anchored to the cardboard, protecting limbs and leaves. With a box cutter, Declan went to work, unwrapping each new delight. An hour later, he stood in a pile of wrappings, admiring his new inventory.

Plants lined the shop. He'd pored over a catalog, picking out those with which he had the greatest confidence as a relative newbie to plant care. There were tropicals, pet-friendly ferns, and some broad-leafed palms. A host of adorable succulents in small containers served a rainbow of pastels. A rick rack cactus dripped over its pot. He'd risked a couple of orchids and a variegated monstera for a showpiece. Declan didn't want to go too wild before he'd had a little practice—and customers—but he'd needed inventory.

When he'd told his mother his plans, she'd suggested it was a phase he'd snap out of, a childish protest. His father changed the subject back to his own conquests. Declan, his youngest son whose purpose seemed to be anything *but* conflict, was a constant disappointment to the patriarch. But his sister had only tilted her head, studied her brother, and said, "I think you'll like them. Quieter than people."

And she was right. Each new plant was a friend. Declan couldn't hold back the smile on his face as he consulted the shipping lists of required care. After ticking off the shipment list, he'd gathered and watered his babies, admiring his collection until a rumble in his gut reminded him to eat.

Declan cleared a spot at the door and unpacked his lunch. Jess had crammed the box with a half dozen tea sandwiches. There was the classic cucumber, a roasted red pepper, and a chicken salad with delicate microgreens. He sat on the remaining barstool, its cracked leather top squeaking as he shifted in the seat, mopping at his mouth with a napkin.

When the afternoon dried out, Declan opened the top half of the door. As he painted, covering a drab taupe with black, he watched for pedestrians passing by the door. Some peeked in the shop, curious about its latest iteration. Others breezed by, involved too deeply in their own worlds to notice the subtle shifts of their surroundings.

Wheels ground against the sidewalk, stopping short of the doorway. Pax slung his arms over the door, leaning in to examine Declan's work.

"Fresh paint?" Pax wore an olive-green bomber jacket, two sizes too big. It bunched around his neck as he judged Declan's work. "Kinda moody in here."

Declan took in the long wall, drying little by little in the mild weather. "You don't like it?"

"Reminds me of Hell's Keep. Like there's a dragon in here or something. And what's with all of these?"

Declan followed Pax's gaze. "The plants? Like I said, it's a plant shop." He empathized with the idle human commentary on teenagers. In Harmonia's books, the main character would bemoan single parenthood of brash teens and would receive hot and heavy comfort from a childless love interest. It was easy to complain about something you'd divorced from your own identity. Declan couldn't remember being a teenager himself, if such a thing had even been possible.

Pax rolled his eyes. "I remember." On the teen's face, Declan saw the old man he would become. He scrunched up his face. "Shouldn't you...uh...you know—put them on tables or something?"

Declan offered his first attempt at sarcasm. "Gee, hadn't thought of that." Noting that Pax leaned further inward on the door, Declan unearthed a massive ginger cookie from within the box and broke it in half. He held the chunk of brown, sugared disk to Pax in an invitation. "Want to check out the place?"

"No way," Pax said, shaking his head. "I know how this turns out. Random guy, a kid like me."

Declan frowned. "Come on, it's not like I'm an axe murderer," he said.

"That's what you'd say if you were one."

"Fair point." Declan sighed. He had to balance kindness with awareness of a potential creep-factor. He took a bite of the cookie. "You're missing out. There's some kind of fancy salt on top of this one. Like big flakey pyramids. Incredible stuff."

Pax watched Declan take another bite before he pushed back from the door. "I'll come in, but if I find out you're some kind of pervy wand-waxer, I'm out."

Wand-waxer? Declan mouthed to himself. He'd add that to the list. For now, he stepped back to what he hoped was a pervert-safe distance as Pax entered the shop.

Pax accepted the cookie half, took a big bite, and squatted in front of some plants. "Fie-cuss lee-ra-ta," he said around his mouthful.

Declan leaned against the bar. "Fiddle leaf fig. A little fussy, I'm told, but happy when established. Don't like to be moved. Or watered too much. Or too little."

"It's pretty," Pax said, hand splaying over one of the large leaves. "But it sounds kinda moody." The teen continued his exploration of the shop's depths. "This place goes on forever," he called from the back. "What are all these rooms?"

Declan had yet to do much with the tiny office, single bathroom, and grimy kitchen. They were next on the ever-growing list of things that should have been done yesterday.

"Helloooo," Maeve called from the door. She stepped over the threshold. "This is looking...serious. Whose skateboard?"

Declan gestured toward the kitchen from where there was a clatter. "A local whose language is baffling. I need a translator for teenspeak. He's either robbing me or deciding if I'm a... wand-waxer."

Maeve snorted. Declan frowned at her reaction. Realization sank in and he blushed. "Oh. *Oh.*"

"Well, are you?"

"Am I a—no!"

Maeve pressed her lips together, stifling a laugh, then gestured to the walls. "I like the color—I do. The plants will pop against this backdrop. Maybe more lights, though?"

"On order," Declan said. "Getting some more shelving built once I figure out what I want. Pax is here giving his expert opinion."

The teen exited the kitchen. "Hey, what's that old machine in the—son of a siren!"

"Son of a—what?"

Pax sighed. "Mom says I swear too much, and it bugs Tim —that's my stepdad. She blames the other gamers."

"Sounds mom-like," Maeve said.

Pax nodded. "But she promised that if I 'upgrade my

language' she'll get me a laptop. Then I could write my own campaigns and—"

"Nerd-out later," Maeve said. She scrutinized Pax. "Why'd you freak out?"

Pax drew his brows down and studied the two adults. "You two are...glowing-like. Different colors. It's kind of weird."

"Glowing?"

"Yeah." Pax pointed at Maeve and then to Declan. "You're purple-y—and younger looking. And you, you've got this... yellow. Well, more gold than anything."

Declan's hands flew to his chest, then to his crotch. He couldn't decide which needed blocking.

Maeve chuckled at Pax's comments. "Must be the bar lights." She turned to Declan. "Can you rig some of these up in my studio? I could use the daily facelift."

Pax continued to stare as he inched his way to the door. He stooped to pick up his board. "I'm gonna find the guys—"

When he was gone, Maeve turned to Declan. "Harmless enough. Interesting about the auras, though. Might be more to that one than I thought."

Declan shrugged. "Auras?"

Maeve brushed his question aside like an abandoned spider web. "All right golden boy, time for yoga. How do you feel about microfibers?"

FIVE

At the studio, Maeve handed him a tangerine *Mudra* shirt and pushed him toward the changing rooms. "Button ups are for stiffs," she said. "We're here to relax."

Declan emerged a few minutes later in an outfit he wanted exactly zero people to ever witness. The bright orange top was snug over his chest, and all his worldly goods were tucked into a pair of tight black shorts. He had a brand-new yoga mat under one arm—a trade with Maeve for one of his cast iron lilies—and a healthy dose of trepidation. This, too, was a novel sensation.

"New here?" The question came from a giant of a man who sported a full, bushy beard, a pair of hot pink microshorts—and little else. Muscles bulged over his body in the tight ropes of a power athlete. His skin had a sheen to it, as though the man had lotioned every inch in preparation for the class. The behemoth grabbed Declan's hand and mashed it within his heavy grip. "You can call me Joe. Welcome to class. Maeve's great. You'll love it."

"Declan, and...thanks." Declan shook out his hand, noting that physical contact with this giant had no effect on the man.

"There's a spot over here," a woman said. She was at the side of the studio, tucked into the back row. She scooted her own mat over to make room for Declan. "Front row is the best for learning, but that last spot's for Cate. She'd murder anyone who takes it. Insists on watching her flow for *meditative* purposes. I think she just wants to check herself out in the mirrors—but that's Cate for you." The woman shrugged. "Anyway, I'm Anastasia."

"Declan. Thanks for the tip—and the spot." When Declan joined her, Anastasia looked away—quickly. She reclined onto her mat like a corpse, eyes closed. Moments later, a willowy woman with cascading hair unrolled her mat in the front spot and proceeded to ogle herself as she stretched.

Declan wasn't sure what to do with his own limbs while he waited for class to start. Some attendees moved through sets of configurations while others lay supine on their mats. Declan attempted a middle ground by lying on his back and pulling a knee to his chest. He promptly rolled over from a lack of balance, releasing his leg and banged his knee on the hard floor. "Gods!" Declan swore through gritted teeth.

Next to him, Anastasia smiled, her eyes remaining closed. "Don't worry, it does get easier."

Maeve entered then, closing the door behind herself with the tinkle of a small bell slung from the knob. She dimmed the lights, then pressed a button on her phone. Soft chanting emanated from speakers parked atop a water cooler. "Welcome, everyone. Whatever baggage you've brought with you today, let's set it aside. This class is for you to embrace the moment. To show yourself compassionate care and kindness. We'll begin seated in a comfortable position, our backs straight."

Declan pretzeled himself into an approximation of

upright calm. He took a deep inhale, noting the pressure riding on his shoulders. In his mind, he packed up the stress of starting over, the pressure from his family, and the feeling of being a fish out of water and set those thoughts next to his mat where they couldn't touch him.

What followed was an hour of Maeve guiding a ragtag group of attendees through a flow that woke every nerve in Declan's body. By the end, he was sweaty, smiling, and thirsty.

Maeve passed him a container labeled Coconut Water as the others filed out into the night.

"Great class," Joe said to Maeve, then clapped Declan on the back. Declan winced at the lighthearted blow. "See you next time?" Joe ducked under the door frame to exit.

"Lovely as always, Maeve," said Cate. The gorgeous woman gave Declan a once-over on her way out. He heard a faint song in the air as she winked at him. "Namaste."

"Thanks, Maeve," Anastasia said, her arms overflowing with workout gear.

"No Phoebe?"

Anastasia shook her head. "Too little sleep. Going back to work has worn her out. Might be a few more weeks." She turned to Declan with a smile. "My niece. She's got a newborn and a bum of a husband. But don't tell her I said that last part."

"Your secret's safe with me." Declan returned her grin. "Good to meet you."

When the last student left, Maeve turned to Declan. "So?"

"I may be dying."

Declan's groin ached in ways he didn't know were possible. His spine was loose and wiggly, though, and he'd discovered the tiny muscles in his feet that weren't his friends—yet. He couldn't remember a time when he'd been aware of every inch of himself.

Maeve clapped her hands together. "Then it worked for you."

Declan nodded. "I think so. Also, I learned that strength does not equal flexibility." He wiped his mouth with the back of his hand. "And that I'm going to need more of this stuff. It's delicious."

The corner of Maeve's mouth turned up. "You'll find it at the co-op." She reached back to flip off the lights in the studio. "I volunteer there for the discount on decent dog food. Got a little pack at home."

Declan downed the rest of the coconut water. "You've got dogs?"

Maeve reached for her coat from a hook. "Scotties. Naughty little beasts, the lot of them, but I love each and every one. I'm a local rescue, of sorts, should you need a companion."

"Not sure a pet would fit my lifestyle," Declan said. "Maybe down the road."

"Suit yourself." Maeve stuffed one arm into a sleeve, then the other. "I'm surprised this is your first yoga class. No studio where you're from?" She peered up at Declan with a knowing look.

Declan shook his head. "Definitely not. Not really a thing there." *Not a lie.*

Maeve locked the door behind them. Declan had changed back into his clothes, his shirt loose at the collar. The night had an edge of chill, but he was still warm from class.

"My place is on the way to yours. Care to escort an old lady to her door?"

∾

Maeve pointed out highlights along their walk. "That place used to be a brothel—a *classy* one, I'm told. This house was one of several they used for court proceedings until the courthouse was built. Rumor has it the basement is haunted—that's where they kept prisoners. We've had more than a couple movies filmed here, too, so it's fun to hunt down those locations if you've got a map and an idle afternoon. And if you squint up that way"—she pointed up the hill—"you'll see the column. Worth the hike if it's sunny."

As they walked, Declan sneaked a peek into windows with lights on in the growing twilight. These were vignettes into the lives of residents who busied themselves over dinner preparations, put in another hour of work in front of a screen, or burped a baby over one shoulder while pacing a room, their lives on display.

Declan strolled alongside Maeve with his new mat wedged under his arm, hands tucked in his pockets. "You know a lot about this place."

"I learn more all the time. It's my adoptive home and I'm partial to it. Astoria is full of secrets, ripe for the digging. Just like people."

Declan stopped in front of a two-story stone house with a deep front porch. A bicycle lay abandoned on the steps. Several plastic flamingos held court in the strip of lawn. Inside, a movie played on a big screen, all animations in bright colors. "What brought you here?" he asked, his eyes watching the scene in front of them.

"Wussed out of a tough situation. Packed up and left. Coward's way out."

Declan turned to look at her, worry etching lines on his face.

"Oh, don't pout on my account," Maeve said. "I'm a big girl. I knew what I was doing."

"Did you...regret it?"

"Do you?" Before he could answer, Maeve started walking again, and Declan followed. "Tell me about your past life.

What did you do before you were master of the plant kingdom?"

"Master? Hah. More like a hopeful apprentice."

"So, it isn't your first job."

Declan sucked in his lower lip. "No. I left a career behind. A predictable career, one in which I ran my own business, and it was steady work."

"Doing what, exactly?" Maeve stopped walking and faced him.

Declan paused, shuffling his feet. He studied the sidewalk for a moment before looking up to answer her. "I was a...counselor. Of sorts."

Maeve lifted an eyebrow. "A psychologist?"

Declan shook his head, chuckling. "Not quite that...serious. I didn't prescribe drugs or anything. I just tried to help people—with their relationships."

"Huh," Maeve said. She was quiet for the next block.

"What about you?"

Maeve looked up at the moon for a moment, then down at her feet. "Used to be in a corporate structure—of sorts," she said, and smiled at Declan. "Top of my game, too. Did I make the right choice? Who's to say," she said, and continued walking. "That was a long time ago. It's done now."

"Why'd you leave?" Declan hadn't meant to sound so lost, but there it was, a crack in his resolve.

"Same reason anyone ever does. Provides a temporary solution to deeper conflicts," Maeve said. She shook her head. "Unresolved issues have a way of rearing their ugly heads down the road, though. No matter how grand your escape."

Declan frowned. Was she talking about her own story...or his? "But what if you don't have another choice? You're backed into a corner and just need—out." Saying the words out loud was freeing, a confession. Declan hadn't said as much to anyone else, not even to his mother when she'd pressed him for rationale. She blamed herself and wailed that she'd failed him. Some of this was true, but he never felt up to saying so, couldn't risk the storms that would follow. He needed space, he'd told her, to figure some things out. Now, he reflected on Maeve's wisdom. Was he running from demons that would find him no matter where he went?

"The idea of starting over is delicious," Maeve said. "Like a forbidden dessert. Some people gorge themselves on the saccharine freshness. But at my age, you know it only leads to a toothache."

Declan chewed on her words as they approached a quaint, cream-colored cottage with a postage stamp-sized yard. A low, white fence bordered the grass. Strings of lights looped from the house out into the trees. On the porch was a rocking chair and a large bowl of water.

"This is me," Maeve said. She unlatched the gate, a rose vine wrapping between its slats. A chorus of barking sounded from within the house. Declan guessed at the location of the couch against the front window as first one, then another furry black face appeared in there, beady brown eyes assessing the arrivals, until the viewpoint was full of judgment.

"Thanks for the history lesson—and the yoga." Declan liked Maeve. As someone with an atypical family dynamic, to have found an ersatz elder was a gift.

"I've got classes running most days of the week if you want to come back. See how sore you are in the morning before you thank me, though," she said, and with a grin, headed up the walk to greet her pack.

Declan flipped on the lights, dropped his keys on the rickety table, and leaned his new yoga mat against the end of his bed. He pulled a bottle of red from his grocery sack and headed back down the stairs. He hadn't gone straight home after Maeve's. Instead, he made a detour to the co-op where he'd loaded up on another box of granola bars, avocados, a loaf of crusty bread, microwave burritos, several jugs of coconut water, and a few bottles of wine.

Bottle in hand, he headed for Jess's front door. Her car was in the driveway, and he hoped she'd want some company. His chat with Maeve stirred up a host of new feelings, all of which left him a bit off-kilter and more than a little lonely. There'd be nothing romantic, he told himself. This was a gesture of friendship, nothing more.

Declan knocked at the door. Stillness. Behind him, a figure shrouded by an umbrella walked an eager lab at the end of a taut leash. Declan counted to ten and knocked again, noting the peeling paint on the doorframe. The sky drizzled. Late summer leaves, made slick with wetness, matted the sidewalks under the streetlamps.

Silence. Declan peered into the front window, the curtain tucked back on one side. The only light was a faint glow from the back hallway.

"Maybe she turned in early," Declan said, and shrugged. "Well, you and I," he said to the bottle, holding it up in the moonlight, "have a date."

Back inside his apartment, he dug in a drawer until he found a wine key from *Mermaid's Lagoon Saloon*. Bottle open, he poured the deep red liquid into a coffee mug and sat by the window ledge. He'd cracked the window open just enough to hear the sounds of the night. His yoga glow, as Maeve had called it, waned as the evening chill sent a rush of goosebumps up his arm. The wine brought its own warmth, however, as he took a sip.

"Not bad," Declan said. He put his feet up on the bed and tilted back in his chair. Through the window, he saw house lights winking out, one by one. Many homes were neutral tones of white, beige, and gray, yet others were cobalt, emerald, and pumpkin. Streetlamps cast an eerie glow as a layer of fog rolled in, cloaking the town. Declan took in this scene, thoughtful.

Playing the part of entrepreneur was a challenge. Running a real business was a new level of complication. Maeve, Jess, and even Sophia made it more than clear how hard they worked. Yet each found satisfaction he wasn't sure was possible working for someone else.

Declan had a plan, a little funding, and a decent location. There was a new to-do list a mile long, though. The painting was finished, but he'd need to find tables, create some kind of decorative theme. Sell the plants he had so he could afford to get more. Keep cleaning and polishing, rearranging and organizing. In the end, it was hard work, but at least it was his.

A jumble of voices shook Declan from his inner monologue. Outside, a heated discussion flamed into an argument. Two voices, one higher, the other deeper. They stopped at the street corner. Declan heard crying, then a shout and the slam of a car door.

Declan straightened his chair, then pressed his ear to the window. From this angle, he couldn't see anyone. He'd thought one voice might be Jess, but whatever violence within the storm had blown over, a soft rain pattering against the windows, but nothing more. The neighborhood was quiet once again.

That night, Declan tossed and turned, spinning his sheets into a cocoon. Insomnia was a new enemy, one that didn't relent until dawn.

Six

Declan woke to a wet spot on his pillow. His drool had soaked through the blue and white stripes. A raging headache pounded between his ears, and as predicted, every inch of his body rebelled against his movement.

The bottle of wine sat two-thirds empty on the table. Wetness slicked the window ledge, and the room was chilly. His phone betrayed a failure to set an alarm—Declan had twenty minutes before he was due to meet Jess's handyman at the Ram & Rose.

"Son of a siren," he said, and rolled out of bed.

Declan dressed in two minutes and had his teeth brushed and a slice of toast crammed down his throat within another five. He hit the pavement as a fresh wave of pressure squeezed his cranium. This was an altogether horrific part of being human, he decided, and sought quick relief.

Coffee. If the line at Pastry House was short, he could almost make it on time to the shop. He sent a text to the contractor to buy a few minutes of forgiveness and tromped down the garage staircase.

Jess's car still sat in the driveway. Declan glanced up at the house. Nothing stirred. He'd peek in at her kitchen downtown —perhaps she'd pulled an all-nighter.

The morning air was crisp and clean. A line of barges waited in the river's mouth, their gargantuan black and red sides reflected on the water. One, laden down with shipping containers, made its way around its sleeping kin. A bald eagle commanded a tower of scaffolding, and pigeons cooed from the rooftops. The morning was cheerful, even if Declan was too worn out to let this sink in.

Pastry House was abuzz. People wedged themselves into every nook, their conversations boisterous. Declan raised his voice over the din to order. "Vanilla latte and a Danish," he said. When a woman broke out in raucous laughter behind him, he winced at the sound. "Busy day," he said to Sophia.

Sophia nodded, filling the portafilter and tamping down the grounds. "It's quiet next door—for once—so people want to stay." She beamed at the crowd as she handed over Declan's breakfast. "Reminds me why I still do this."

Declan tipped his cup to her and breezed out the door, eager to distance himself from the jostling and volume. Those behind him in line had pressed up against his back, taking every opportunity to touch him, and he could swear a woman pinched his rear on his way out of the shop. Jess's door was locked. Declan shaded his gaze with one hand against the glare to peer into the kitchen, but the space was unoccupied.

Back on the pier, Declan spotted a woman sitting on the end, legs dangling over the edge. She looked a lot like Cate, her caramel-colored hair streaming in the breeze. Her eyes tracked something in the water below, a gull perched next to her on the railing. With a time check, Declan dismissed the urge to move closer and picked up his pace.

Outside the Ram & Rose, a man held a tape measure to

his front window. "Casing's rotted," he said, as soon as Declan was within earshot.

"Thanks for coming. I didn't get to meet you the other day. I'm Declan."

The man nodded. "Aiden Sturrock, but most call me Sturrock. Been a Sturrock in Astoria since its inception."

"Oh, uh...that's good?" Thanks to the coffee, the thudding in Declan's skull had quieted. "I appreciate you coming by."

"It's not a bad location," Sturrock said. "If you don't mind the eau de skunk from down the block." The man continued his measuring, jotting notes on a clipboard in hand. "People can say what they want about that kind of business, but they did a big remodel when they moved in. Spruced it up. This place, though..." Sturrock said, running a tongue across his front teeth, "hasn't changed since it was built. In case you're wondering, that's not a good thing—but it's got decent bones."

"That *is* why I hired you," Declan said through his teeth. His patience stretched, he grabbed the doorknob, prepared to insert his key in the lock. The top half of the door swung inward. Had he forgotten to latch it last night? Declan unlocked the bolt and pressed inside, Sturrock close on his heels. Both men froze when they saw the shop's interior.

The plants were fine, though a few had toppled, soil scattered across the floor. Gone were the neat rows Declan arranged for categorization. The ancient cash register remained behind the bar, and Declan's stack of paperwork waited, organized by pressing need, on the counter. Everything was fine—except the walls.

On the fresh black paint and sprayed across the wide mirror over the bar were several looming, amateur depictions of a size and shape possible only in a fictional state.

"But they're all giant—" Sturrock's jaw slackened as he stared at the drawings.

"Yeah." Declan's voice was steady while heat boiled in his chest.

"And they're...spray painted. Yellow—no, *gold*."

"Yeah."

Sturrock lifted his chin as though to take in the artwork from a different angle. "I don't think they have a lot of experience with these. The proportions are all—"

Declan huffed and turned away from the walls. "Can we please get to the estimate? It's clear I have a cleanup job ahead of me."

Sturrock pressed his lips together and returned to his clipboard. He walked Declan through the space, noting which improvements were immediate and which could stand to wait. All the while, he snuck glances at the anatomical display sprayed on the walls for all to see.

"So, when can you start?" Declan had agreed to rewiring, new piping, and the construction of shelves. Refinishing the bar would have to wait, as would the floors.

"Next week works, if that will give you enough time to... ah..." Sturrock gestured over Declan's shoulder. "Repaint."

"They'll be gone today," Declan promised, as Joe ducked his head below the doorway to join them.

"Wow, that's an interesting choice," the man said. "Wouldn't have pegged you as someone into the male—"

"Bananas?" Anastasia peeked in behind Joe. They were both dressed in yoga attire. Joe pushed back the door for Anastasia, who stepped farther into the shop. When she took in the entirety of the graffiti, her eyes went wide. "Oh. *Oh*. Those are—"

Declan put his hands over his face. "Should I invite *everyone* in for a peep?" *This isn't happening,* he told himself. This was a dream brought on by too much wine and nostalgia.

A low whistle echoed in the shop. Cate joined them from the doorway. "Who decked out this place in—"

"Don't say it," Declan commanded. "You'll make it worse."

"Son of a siren!" Pax gawped at the scene, skateboard in hand.

"I need to keep that door closed," Declan muttered, his mortification complete.

Joe scratched his head. "I dunno. It is kind of funny. Not every day you get to see—"

"Nothing," Declan said. "You see nothing. I'm going to paint over them, and we're all going to forget we ever saw anything on these walls. Better add change the locks to that list," he added to Sturrock.

"It's a shame," Sturrock said. "Someone did this. Downtown's going to the dogs. Better make a police report."

"Police?" Pax's eyes went wide. He edged his way back toward the door.

Cate blocked his exit. "The innocent don't run," she said, and he froze. "You wouldn't know who did this, would you?"

Pax shook his head. "Why should I know?"

"Just asking," Cate said, her eyes narrowing. "Wouldn't want Declan's new shop ruined by a crew of scallywags."

"I'll help you paint," Joe said. "My columns are in for the week, so I've got the afternoon off. Maeve will understand." The man wore a brewery sweatshirt over his bulk and had a strip of leather wrapped around one massive wrist. At his neck, he wore a slice of pinecone dipped in resin, the seeds spiraling outward in a hypnotizing pattern. Joe brushed past Declan to don a smock, the stretch of fabric covering his chest like a bikini top. He collected a paint roller and tray from the stack of supplies in the back and went to work opening a can.

"Monday morning," Sturrock said. He nodded at the

others, and with a last look at the walls, headed back out, Pax following behind.

Cate turned a slow circle, a smile playing at her lips. "You know, for all the access to personal inspiration, no one seems to get them quite right, do they?"

Declan stifled a chuckle of his own. The situation was ridiculous.

"See you in class?" Cate batted her eyelashes at Declan and waved. He spotted a giant rock on her ring finger. "Shame you aren't planning to keep them. Kind of avant-garde, if you ask me."

"Perhaps I should frame a picture of them for you."

"I'd like that," Cate said, her laughter the sound of crystal chimes. She bent down to pick up a potted fern. Its rippled fronds stretched out from the center. "And this. Reminds me of seaweed." She removed a wad of bills from her sparkly yoga top, peeled some off, and placed the money on the bar. "Thanks!"

When she'd left, Joe stood up from his crouched position. He'd coated the roller in black and went to work on the yellow paint in slow, easy strokes. "Easy there," he said, maintaining a steady rhythm. "She's a live one. And according to her, taken."

"Thanks for the heads up," Declan said. "But I'm not looking."

Joe continued his strokes. "Oh? Got a girl—or a guy— back home?"

Declan shrugged. "It's complicated, but no. Not anymore."

The duo painted in companionable silence until the walls were again blank and black. When Joe left, Declan attacked the mirror with a razor. He would need to add cameras to his growing list, an expensive addition. In a box under his bed lay Declan's two remaining treasures, but he didn't want to sell those, too. Not yet.

The walk home was somber. Declan's feet dragged up the driveway. He'd eaten a half bag of chips and an underripe avocado for lunch, too focused on his task list to stop for a proper meal. Between that and the coffee he'd inhaled like water, his gut was a mess. If this was the dark side of being human, he had complete empathy for the poor creatures.

In the driveway, Declan frowned at Jess's car. She'd said she had some downtime later that week, but hadn't she promised to stop by the shop? He rounded the house toward the front porch. Maybe she was taking a well-deserved day off. Declan listened for the familiar operatic notes, but there came none from the house. He paused at the bottom of the porch steps.

Declan gnawed at his lower lip. He should stay out of it. This was too forward. She was his landlord, and he was her tenant. For all he knew, she had a lover upstairs, and they'd spent a day indulging in each other. The images painted on the shop walls flashed in his mind, and he shook his head, irritated. This day had been far too long. He should call her first. Or maybe just text. He'd say hi and confirm that she could stop by the shop whenever she liked. He pulled out his phone and headed for the garage.

In the yard, a flutter of fabric caught Declan's eye. As he approached, the coffee and avocado roiled in his stomach and he retched in the grass.

There, between two ancient rhododendrons, their spring flowers long since spent and dried, was a pile of nightclothes, stained with red.

A figure was splayed out beneath the bushes, limbs stretched out like a starfish. The small body lay in the grass, the terrycloth soaking in residual dew. Straps of a bathrobe flung outward from its owner, the billowy fabric obstructing the face. There was no question, however, to whom the robe belonged.

Declan called the police.

While he stood, staring, emergency personnel swarmed into the yard from all sides, their radio chatter becoming white noise in his mind, some in black uniforms, others in blue. Flashing lights along the block, a crowd huddled on the sidewalk, whispering. Declan was the eye of the storm, a steadfast observer of the chaos and humanity that rolled forward like a three-dimensional movie screened just for him. When they left, her body on a stretcher, zipped into a black plastic bag, it was as though a vacuum sucked all the air from the place. Police tape stretched over the front porch and the back door to the house, the yellow and black plastic ends snapping in the wind like a kite's tail.

How could this have happened, and when? These two questions fought for answers in the depths of his mind. He wracked his brain for anything that would make sense of the horror he'd seen, the gut punch of the discovery. But there was none. This was a tragedy, and Declan was crushed.

An officer followed Declan to the garage steps, grilling him on his whereabouts, the victim's habits, anything out of the ordinary Declan may have seen. Declan, numb, gave brief answers to his questions. The officer insisted Declan sleep elsewhere that night and pressed a card into his hand. "If you think of anything," he said, "call me. I'm sure the family will be in touch."

Declan spent the evening staring out his shop window, unmoored by his new sense of justice.

Seven

The next afternoon, Declan stood at the bar, transcribing tags for each plant. Each bamboo tag had the common name on one side and the scientific name with a price listed on the back. Declan concentrated on his handwriting, warring against the exhaustion that tugged at his eyelids.

His sleep, what little Declan scrounged curled up in one of the booths, was fitful at best. He'd struggled against the sensations of guilt, shame, and loss. He dreamed the house called to him, music swelling from within until the windows burst out in a symphony of shattering glass.

That morning he'd sold a hoya and a geranium to a woman who'd carried them out under her arms like children. The owner of the Italian restaurant stopped by to put in an order for tabletop arrangements. Each transaction provided a momentary distraction from his grim reality.

"Knock knock," Cate called at the door. Her voice was soft and somber.

"Come in," Declan said, without turning from his work.

"I brought the gang," Cate added.

Declan looked up and into the mirror in front of him. Cate entered with Maeve, Joe, and Anastasia following behind.

"We brought your favorite," Maeve said, plunking down a container of coconut water. "And wanted to see how you're holding up."

"Looking good." Joe let out a low whistle. "I love what you've done with the place. Modern, yet natural." He fingered a spider plant pup dangling from the mother plant.

"It's really coming along," Anastasia said.

Declan rubbed at the back of his neck. "Thanks. Pax helped a bit, and it will make a little more sense when the shelves are up. But...yeah. It's coming along."

"What's this one?" Cate ran a finger along a flowering stem. "It's so pretty."

"Bleeding hearts," Declan said. "They're herbaceous."

"Sounds like the name of an advice column," Joe added.

"Adding one to the *Astorian*? Could shake some life into that paper," Anastasia said.

Joe picked up a cactus with a bushy white crown. "Might not be a bad idea. We could definitely use the readers."

"You know, Declan used to give advice," Maeve said, leaning against the bar. Declan shot her a look, but she continued. "*Love* advice."

"Really?" Cate asked. She flipped a lock of hair over her shoulder. "Sounds scandalous."

"Sometimes," Declan said. "But not always. Can be sad, too."

Joe took the stool next to Declan. The seat groaned under his weight. "Tell me more."

Declan shrugged. "It was...just what I did. I mean, people need a little help sometimes, that's all."

Joe prodded. "Can you write?"

Declan gestured to the tags in front of him. "Like this?"

"As in, could you get me five hundred words by Monday?"

"Five hundred—but I don't have anyone to advise."

Anastasia puffed out a breath. "I could use some advice," she muttered. Joe lifted his brows as if in interest or agreement.

"Better make that two articles. The editor might like one more than the other. Two boosts your chances of getting published."

Cate nodded. "This is a brilliant plan. All the who's-who of Astoria have disastrous love lives. There's a certain council member who's a new daddy but his wife doesn't know, rich singletons who fall for catfishing scams—and that doesn't even touch my friends at the club who claim they've 'grown apart' from their spouses but everyone knows it's just a cover. *Everyone* has trouble with love."

No joke, thought Declan. *Me, too.*

"I know," Maeve said. "We'll put up a sign outside the studio. On the bulletin board. People are tired of staring at the same business cards. Something like this will snap up their attention."

"On the sidewalk board? I don't know, Maeve," Anastasia said. "Seems kind of...public."

Joe scratched at his beard. "There's no requirement to include a real name. No need to reveal whose dirty laundry we read."

"What if you help people find true love?" Cate had a dreamy look. She bounced on the balls of her feet. "Or what if it gets spicy?"

Maeve waved her off. "Won't know until we try it."

"We've already got a name for the column," Joe said, touching the delicate strand of petals with the tip of his finger. "Bleeding Hearts."

Declan grimaced. "That might put people off. Seems a bit —intense."

"No, *we're* the Bleeding Hearts," Cate said. "Since we'll have to read through all of them and take on the drama of the whole town. We have to help Declan pick the best questions, right?"

"*Get* to read them?" Maeve raised an eyebrow at Cate.

Joe nodded in slow confirmation. "An editorial board. This could really work."

Anastasia tapped a finger against her chin. "A club of sorts. I like it."

Cate paced the room, thinking aloud. "We vet the questions and Declan...well," Cate waved her hand around in the air, "works his romance magic, whatever that is. The lovesick get advice and readers get entertainment. It's perfect!"

"We'll call it Dear Declan. It'll be a weekly piece," Joe said. He snapped his fingers in the air several times. "Ideas are popping—this is great."

"What can I say?" Maeve whispered in Declan's ear as the others buzzed over the column's potential. "You needed a distraction."

Declan opened his mouth to reply when Cate clapped her hands together. "This is great! All we need now are some victims."

"Been here two days and you're already a criminal."

"Shove off, Maeve," Declan said. "I didn't do it."

Maeve handed him another plant to hang from the repurposed coat rack salvaged from the office. "Ah, but that's what you'd say if you had done it."

"I'm not in the mood for this. To be honest, I'm surprised you are."

Maeve sighed. "Mourning doesn't help the dead. Jess was a

lovely woman who has gone far too soon. But don't throw your time away because hers is up."

"I know you're right, but I can't get the picture of her out of my mind. She was just so...broken."

Maeve handed him the last of the plants in hanging pots. Declan had rigged one of the new grow lights to the underside of the topmost rung. The contraption didn't look half bad. He was eager for Sturrock to build some permanent fixtures, but this was a solid, temporary fix.

"Coming to class?"

"Can't," Declan said, though he didn't meet her eye. "An officer is coming by to grill me—on my whereabouts."

Declan was anxious about the investigation. The last thing he needed was to be questioned about his past and where-abouts. Even if he could spin a plausible backstory, any invasion of his privacy was a risk. Each time he considered the line of questions, he got queasy.

He'd seen dead people before, thousands of them—that came with his heritage. However, the loss of life hadn't sunk within his soul before. In fact, he wasn't sure he'd had a soul before now.

"Suit yourself," Maeve said. "My door's always open."

Declan wiped down the inside of the beverage cooler, disassembled the four broken stools to cobble together two complete versions, and was busy waxing the bar when the officer entered. He abandoned his rag on the bar, steeling himself for whatever came next.

"Looking good," the man said. "Better than it ever did, actually."

Aside from the second coat of fresh plant paint, Declan had hung a set of black and white photographs of leaves he'd thrifted that morning. The place smelled of pine-scented cleaner and he'd polished up the register. "Thanks, Officer... uh?"

The man pointed to his uniform. "Rooney. And you must be Declan Rosewood?" He withdrew a notepad from one of his many pockets.

Declan nodded and gestured to the repaired stools. "Water? I'm afraid that's all I've got."

"I'm good. So, uh...Mr. Rosewood. You've already detailed what happened the night you found Ms. Black at her residence, which is also your residence...is that right?"

"Yes. Well, no," Declan began. "I mean, yes, I gave a statement about that night. No to the part where we share a residence. Mine is separate. The apartment over the garage."

"I see," said the man. He pursed his lips, considering Declan. "So, you never went over to her house?"

"I've been in her house before."

"You have? And you reported this?"

Declan frowned. "I did."

Detective Rooney scribbled furiously on the notepad. "Can you tell me the details of when you visited Ms. Black in her home?" He stared hard at Declan. A tiny muscle in Rooney's lower eyelid twitched.

"Monday. Once to get my keys and then again later that evening."

"That evening?"

"Yes, Monday evening." Declan watched the man's cheeks purple, his building anger laid bare.

"Did you talk to her in the house?"

"It would have been weird to shout at her through the doorway."

Rooney shifted his jaw. "What was the nature of your relationship with Ms. Black?" The officer leaned so far forward Declan thought the man might fall off the stool.

"She was my landlord. I only met her two days ago."

"I see." Rooney consulted his pad. "Would you say you found Ms. Black attractive?"

Declan recoiled. "Excuse me?" Being questioned by a human was a novel experience, but Declan's sense of self-preservation had officially kicked in.

"Were you engaged in any kind of flirtation with Ms. Black? Have you ever approached her? Been rejected, perhaps?"

"This is over," Declan said. He hopped off his stool and crossed to the door. "I'm calling a lawyer." Declan didn't have a lawyer, but this was what characters said when grilled by authorities in the movies.

"Now, now," the detective said, pocketing his notebook. "No need to get upset. You've got to admit, when a stranger moves into town and his landlord winds up dead, people will have questions. Ms. Black was a pillar of our community, and we protect our own."

"I won't be admitting anything," Declan said, holding the door open. He gestured outward toward the street in case the situation required further clarity.

Rooney shook his head as he left. "We could have done this the easy way. I'll be in touch."

Declan said nothing. His face was an ice block, devoid of expression. When the officer ducked back in his cruiser, Declan collapsed into the doorway.

A chorus of wheels on pavement shook him from his stupor. Two skaters whizzed by, their riders employing deft movements to avoid pedestrians and the city trash bins painted with vintage cannery designs. A third rider skidded to a stop in front of Declan.

"Hey, Pax," Declan said. Somehow the presence of the teen was comforting.

"Hey." The boy stood next to his board, eyeing his feet.

Pax remained silent, so Declan prodded. "Coming to confess?"

Pax lifted his face, his green eyes wide and incredulous. "What?"

"About the paint job."

"How did you—? I mean, it wasn't me. Honest."

Declan jerked his chin toward the retreating skaters. "It was them, wasn't it?"

Pax bit his lower lip and looked away. He nodded, a silent acknowledgment.

"You didn't do it, but you told them about my place." Declan's ability to sense true emotions was a mere fraction of its former strength, but anyone could spot a squirming teenager when they saw one. "How'd they get in?"

"Butter knife," Pax said.

That explained the unlatched top half of the door. "That break-in cost me a couple hours of my time and a bucket of paint. What are your thoughts on that?"

Pax glanced down the street at his friends, then past Declan and into the shop. "Don't have any money. But I could help you for a bit."

"I'd like that," Declan said.

He put Pax to work scrubbing down the kitchen. The boy sobered, intent on his work. In truth, Declan was glad for the company. The officer's questions left him shaken.

When Pax left, gleaming stainless steel in his wake, Declan wanted to be anywhere but alone. Two doors down from the darkened Mudra was a sports bar that served fish, chips, and double shots of tequila. Declan ate and drank too much, a murderous combination. When the bartender asked if there was anyone they could call, in his inebriated state, Declan could name only one person.

"Don't worry, Ted, I'll pour him into bed. I know where

he lives," Maeve assured the bartender. She looped one of Declan's arms around her neck. "Come on, golden boy. I can't do all the work."

"Thanksh for thish, May—Mavis—Maeve." Declan's words slurred. "You're a real...a real...well, anyway, thanksh."

Maeve waited for the crosswalk sign to light up before stepping off the curb with Declan in tow. "I expect you to do the same for me someday."

"Anytime," Declan said, then stumbled. The traffic lights swam in his vision like birds in a blackened sky. "Except maybe not tonight."

"Don't worry, I'm stone cold sober. Alcohol plus hot yoga is a terrible idea."

They walked another block, Maeve half dragging Declan. She was shorter, but strong for her size. "You're one tough lady, Maeve."

"Aging is no joke. I like to face her head-on."

"You're pretty great, you know," Declan said, a moment of clarity piercing the fog within his brain. "Were you always a yog-gah...yo-guy...yo-goo..."

Maeve corrected. "Yogi?" Declan nodded, his head lolling. She continued. "Nope, it's a recent thing. Helped me deal with the past, though. Leave it all on the mat and whatnot."

Declan lifted his chin to look at the moon. Its silvery face beamed out from between the clouds. "Feels like my past was nothing *but* stress."

Maeve stopped to redistribute Declan's weight. "Tell me more."

"Seems stupid, now." Declan shook his head, reeled from the movement, and steadied himself again. "I got caught up in other people's...drama," he began again. Declan tried to focus as faces flooded his memory. "I tried to help. Every day I tried. But in the end, I'm just a hack."

"I don't believe that for a minute," Maeve said, checking

both ways before guiding Declan across the street. "Most of us could use a kick in the pants with our love lives. Someone like you to help us see past our own ego. Bet you had a line down the block."

"But—" A great sob escaped Declan's lips. "The last person I gave advice to was Jess!" Like opening a floodgate, once Declan started, it flowed in a great hiccuping storm of emotion.

Maeve patted him on the shoulder. "Come now," she said. "I'm sure whatever you told her, she needed to hear. That girl had the worst luck with men. None of them were doing her any favors."

"I'm no good to anyone." Declan sniffled into her shoulder. "What am I even doing here?"

"Here?"

"In Astoria," Declan wailed. His heart was raw, the words tumbling out in a newfound waterfall of feeling. "What made me think I could run a plant shop? I can't even run my own life. Existence. Life. Whatever you'd call—"

"Shh now," Maeve said, glancing around. "No need to spill our secrets on the streets. Let's get you home."

Declan trudged up the hill, leaning hard into Maeve, sweat beading at his brow. "Home? Bah. I'll be lucky if they don't throw me out in a week."

At the house, Declan vomited in the driveway before Maeve wrestled him up the stairs and into the apartment where he collapsed on the bed in a heap. She tugged off his shoes and set a glass of water on the side table before pulling the duvet over his limp body. After placing some aspirin on the table, she patted his shoulder. "We struggle most when we go against our nature. Leverage your strengths, my friend, don't fear them…and stay away from tequila."

Eight

Declan had two goals for the day: study plant care and avoid arrest.

On his way to work, he'd stopped by the Pastry House, busy as ever.

With breakfast, he'd picked up a copy of the paper. The *Astorian* published a brief article on the tragic death of the local caterer, Jessica Black, stating that an investigation into the circumstances was ongoing. Anyone with information was to contact the police department.

Declan snapped the newspaper taut when he found the obituaries.

Jessica Black, 31, a renowned Astoria businesswoman, died at her home after a life lived honoring the community with her divine dishes and warm personality. Her dedication to supporting our local food bank with meal preparation and management will not be forgotten. A service will be held at Our Lady of Lourdes. In lieu of flowers, please donate to the food bank in Jessica's name...

White noise swallowed Declan. He sat at one of the tiny tables in Pastry House, rereading the text.

"What has you in its clutches?" Sophia asked. She'd ventured out from behind the counter to wipe down the abandoned tables.

Declan sighed. "A short story. Far too short." He set the paper down and tipped the last of his coffee down his throat.

Sophia peered at the paper. Her face blanched, and she turned away, hurrying to finish the tables.

Declan pushed back his chair and made his way to the front door. Through the glass, he watched two officers pass. One was Rooney, the other was a burly man with a ginger beard and ruddy cheeks. Declan ducked in reflex, though neither man looked his way.

After counting to fifty, Declan checked the sidewalk. Empty. Down the block sat a patrol car. He slipped out the front door and hurried down the street. On the way past Jessica's old kitchen, he spared a glance through the window. An oversized calendar hung on the wall, her handwriting spread across the month with orders penciled-in. That Sunday had a red circle around the date with a note—*Wedding pitch*—and the following Friday had the term *Date* penciled in.

At the street corner, Declan looked back. There was no sign of anyone, official or otherwise, following him. He turned around to hit the crosswalk button only to bump right into Cate.

Cate dropped her purse, its contents spilling over the sidewalk.

"I'm so sorry," Declan said, scrambling to catch an aluminum can before it rolled into the street. "I didn't see you."

"No, it's my fault," Cate said, shaking her head, "Walking and texting—I know better." She stooped to scoop up a large white comb. Its surface shimmered.

Declan handed her the can. "Tuna fan?"

"Lunch," she said with a shrug and nervous laugh. She dropped the can back in her purse. "You know how it is when your days are always go, go, go. Thanks again!"

"Sure," Declan said, noting the brush off. "Wait, you missed something." He picked up a navy container from the welcome mat of the bookstore. He looked at the familiar label. "Is this your salt?"

"Haha, yes, well. Grew up with it, you know? Can't abide by the cheap stuff." Cate jammed the canister back into her bag, a shimmery green tote covered in sequins that sparkled in the morning sunlight. "See you later!"

Declan watched as she hurried to the boardwalk. When he checked the other direction, the patrol car was gone. He continued his walk, alert.

At Ram & Rose, he found Pax leaning against the doorjamb. The boy thrust a brown paper sack in Declan's direction. "From Mom," he said.

Declan frowned. "Your mother?" The top of the bag was crinkled, the consequence of travel. He unrolled the crumpled paper, and the scent of brown sugar and toasted oats greeted him. A dozen cookies lined the bottom of the sack. He withdrew one and inhaled its fresh-baked smell before chomping down.

"Came clean about the...graffiti. Then told her I confessed and helped you out, but she grounded me anyway. Said she was proud I did the right thing in the end, though." Pax shrugged. "Moms."

"Yeah," Declan said, thinking of his own mother and her reactions to his decision-making. "Please tell her these are delicious. Might be my lunch today."

Pax smiled from underneath his shaggy locks and mounted his skateboard. As he wheeled away, he saluted Declan.

Declan opened the door of the shop and was walloped by a wave of warm, humid air. The wall of oxygen welcomed him, dense and full of promise. He stopped to admire a new leaf in one pot, a flower bud in another. His collection was now labeled and categorized by lighting and watering needs. Declan checked the beverage cooler, running empty for two days for stability. The inside was cold and crisp. He could officially order flowers but pushed that to the back of his mental list.

A new tool chest waited on the bar, its drawer filled with a starter set of hammers, pliers, and other items he'd collected. Declan removed four black nails from the box and climbed onto the back counter of the bar. He marked the wall above the mirror with an X, hammered in one nail and then another. Two more nails and the job was done.

"Boss said it's a go," Joe said, pushing in the lower door to enter the shop. He held half a ham and cheese sandwich in one hand, a pencil in the other. "Whatcha doing?"

Declan looked from the hammer in his hand, his backpack on the counter, and then to Joe. "Uh...hammering."

Joe gave a quick nod. "Right on."

A chunk of ham fell from the sandwich onto Joe's beard. Declan grimaced. "You've got something...just there—" He pointed at the offending bit.

Joe stopped chewing and looked down at his chest, causing the ham to fall to the floor. "Don't see it. Anyway. The column. It's yours if you want it."

"Right, the column. Of course." Declan bit his lip. He itched to take on the job, but he worried he wouldn't have the same influence he once held. Declan was used to intervention over written instruction. "Any rules to the gig?"

"Five hundred words and make it good. If it's not, they'll cut the column. You'll get paid if it runs."

Declan nodded. "Seems fair."

"Maeve put a sign up," Joe said. "A few folks are reading it just now. One took a card. Cross your fingers that our first official meeting of the Bleeding Hearts will take place tonight."

Declan paged through a book on terrariums. According to the authors, any container could become a miniature world of its own, complete with tiny plants and even poison dart frogs. Declan didn't trust himself with a shop full of amphibians, but he adored the miniature, controlled environments pictured on the glossy pages. He considered the back end of the shop where an old booth remained. Customers could assemble their own terrariums in the shop if he repurposed that nook. He'd pick up some glass canisters in one of the thrift shops and the plants would be easy enough to source.

"Hello—" Anastasia entered the shop, a cloth sack in hand. "Brought you something. You might not want them, but in case..." She set the bag on the counter and opened the drawstring.

Declan looked up from his reading to peer into the bag. "Empty shells?"

"Hazelnuts. To protect the soil," Anastasia said. "You use them for mulch—help with drainage, too. No worries if you don't want them. My sister's got loads on her farm, though, so I thought I'd offer."

"Thanks," Declan said, hefting the sack to his potting table. "Might help the palms."

"I'm also using them as an excuse." Anastasia locked eyes with Declan. She blinked a few times, then looked away. "To talk about Jess."

"Jess?"

"And the column," Anastasia added. She studied her feet. "We got excited yesterday. I think we kind of steamrolled you

into it. You just saw a body—Jessica, someone we all knew—
and there we were, obsessing over the potential dirt on
people's love lives. People handle grief differently and well...I
just wanted to say that it's totally okay to say no. Maeve'll
come up with some other wild scheme. Always does," Anastasia said. "Anyway, we can be a lot, all at once. Don't take us
too seriously."

Declan had the urge to hug the woman. Someone had put
his feelings first. "I appreciate that," he said. "You can't know
how much. But I'd like to try the column. Might be good for
me. Maybe even drum up some business for the shop."

Anastasia nodded. "Good. See you after class?"

"I'll be there." Anastasia latched the lower half of the door
behind her when Declan called to her. "Anastasia?"

She paused in the doorway. "Yeah?"

"You don't think Jess would have...well...done anything on
purpose, do you?"

Anastasia looked at her hands where they rested on the
lower door. She shook her head. "It crossed my mind, I admit.
But there's just no way. She didn't have an easy life, but she
loved the one she had. You should have seen how proud Jess
made her grandmother before Zelda died. Jess carried a legacy,
and she wouldn't have given that up."

Declan frowned. "An article in the *Astorian* mentioned an
investigation."

"I should hope so," Anastasia said, meeting his gaze. "Her
death makes zero sense, no matter which way you look at it."

Declan drew his brows together, then risked the question
looming in his mind. "You don't think *I* did it, do you?"

Anastasia's answer was quick. "No," she said. "What
would you have gained?"

Declan exhaled all the air in his lungs. "Thanks for the
faith. I'm under the impression that a certain police officer has
me pegged as a suspect."

"I wouldn't take it too personally. In fact, I'd be upset if they didn't question you and everyone else." She toyed with a necklace above her collar, sliding a small anchor pendant along the silver chain. "Listen. There are people in this town who don't like outsiders," she said. "Don't let them get to you."

Declan checked the message board outside of Mudra. Someone—he narrowed that list to four suspects—had crafted a poster that read:

> Free love advice!
>
> Get your biggest questions answered by a professional and published in a brand-new column in the *Astorian*! Fill out a card with your heart's wonderings and post it here. Add your name or stay anonymous. Subscribe to the paper and stay tuned!

An envelope tacked under the poster held a handful of business cards near a pencil dangling from a ribbon. He breezed past the poster, a flutter of excitement in his chest.

For the second time in a week, Declan found himself in too tight pants, staring at his uncomfortable self in a line of giant mirrors. Tonight's class added a few other townsfolk to Maeve's lesson. She'd daubed their palms with ylang ylang oil, instructed them to rub the mixture on the bottoms of their feet, then invited all to join her in Mountain pose.

The key, Maeve told them, was to ground oneself through pressing firmly with all ten toes. Declan attempted this, yet teetered, unbalanced.

"Draw your navel in, but keep your knees soft. If you pass out from trying too hard, I'll do my best to catch you, but no promises," she whispered, and winked at Declan in the mirror.

After class, the Bleeding Hearts waited for the rest of the students to leave. Street lamps winked on, the dark sinking in earlier with the advancing season.

"Okay, okay," Cate squealed. "It's been long enough. Let's check the board!"

Declan, Maeve, Joe, Anastasia, and Cate trooped to the door of the studio.

"I see one!"

NINE

"Every time I get my hair cut, my stylist compliments me and tells me how attractive I look. Are they hitting on me or just saying that for tips? Trying to figure out if I should ask them out," Cate read. "They signed it Silent Salon Admirer."

Anastasia reached for the card. "I appreciate the context."

"I say go for it," Cate said. "That one's too easy."

Maeve poured from a box of wine into everyone's now empty water bottles. "Hang on a minute. We just got started. Let's give this our full consideration."

Joe retrieved two protein bars from his duffel bag and broke them into chunks. He handed out the pieces. "I agree. Let's savor our first lonely soul."

"Well, we can narrow things down a bit, see if that helps. There are only two salons." Anastasia took a sip. "Salon Nouveau and Chopped."

Joe made a face. "Wait a sec, what about Curl Up and Dye?"

Cate shook her head. "The stylists there are married and bitter gossips."

"Are we ignoring the barber shop?"

Anastasia grimaced. "Enzo's got to be in his eighties by now. Not sure he's looking to date. But maybe?"

Maeve extracted a bag of pistachios from a cabinet and set it in the middle of their gathering. They'd circled cushions on the studio floor, stacking a few foam blocks to form a makeshift table.

Declan reached for a pistachio. He used the tips of his fingers to pry open the shell, then popped the morsel in his mouth and chewed. "Tasty," he said, and reached for more. No matter the era, people loved food and drink at every gathering.

"That's all our famous love expert has to say?" Anastasia teased.

Declan took a sip of the wine, a compliment to the salty snack. The box decried a red blend that complemented the saltiness. He wondered if his old buddy Di would approve.

Maeve watched him as he took another sip. "Never had boxed wine before...or is it the nuts?"

Declan studied her, a smile on his lips. "Not together, that's for sure." Her tone was light, jesting, yet there was something behind her question.

"Come on," Joe said. He scratched at his tree trunk thighs. "Don't hold out on us."

Cate whipped out her lipstick and approached the mirror. "We've got to stay organized, people."

"I don't like the look of this..." Maeve said.

Cate brushed her off. She uncapped the tube and twisted out a red cylinder. "It'll be fine, it's washable. Besides, George slid his sweaty feet up this one and there's streaks."

"Fine, fine," Maeve said, shaking her head. "But I'll need more wine if it's getting serious."

Cate drew a t-chart and put a salon name at the top of

each column. With deft strokes of the cherried hue, she listed sets of initials.

Anastasia studied the list. "How do you know all the stylists?"

"A girl with hair like mine doesn't mess around. Can't trust these locks with just anyone."

Anastasia rolled her eyes skyward in an exaggerated gesture, then smiled at Cate. "All right, proceed."

"Well," Cate said, adopting the pose of an instructor. She capped the lipstick and employed it as a pointer. "We can draw lines through three of them at least. It's not Caryn, Liz, or Jamison. They're all way too grouchy."

"And Jamison is married," Joe piped up.

"Doesn't necessarily rule someone out," Declan said. The cheap wine warmed him from the inside out. After the deep stretching, he was in a satisfied state of relaxation. He recrossed his legs and leaned forward, excited by the analysis.

"Fair," Joe said. He scratched again, catching Declan's eye. "Appointment with the aesthetician tomorrow," he whispered, as though this made sense.

"Still, I'm going to cross out Donna," Cate said, running the edge of the tube through the initials D. L. "She's cheerful, but there's no way she's looking."

Anastasia groaned. "Yes. That woman isn't allowed to complain—ever."

Maeve laughed. "She's the worst."

Confused, Declan asked, "What am I missing?"

"Husband's a firefighter," Maeve said. "Women—and men—fall all over him. Everyone's a bit jealous."

Declan nodded. "Got it."

"I'm not jealous," Cate said, arms crossed. "Jack is my one, true love."

"Yours and two others'," Anastasia said, taking a drink.

Cate glared at Anastasia. "Because your love life is so hot."

"Enough," Maeve said. "We all envy that headboard, and you both know it."

Declan lifted his brows. "Okay, this I've got to hear."

Anastasia sighed. "Donna rekindled things with Keith a year ago. He was her old high school sweetheart and they eloped. Neighbors keep calling in noise complaints."

"Oh my," Declan said. "Young love."

"They're in their fifties," Maeve said, a wry smile on her face.

Declan slapped his knee. "Even better!"

"So, who's left?" Anastasia stood to consult the list. "Is A.J. Anita Johnson? She cuts my hair."

"I've got her and Ray left at Chopped—and Jamison."

"It's not Anita," Anastasia said. She reached for the tube and scratched a line through the red streaks. "Keeps her distance from her customers. Once a client sent her a dozen roses tied with a lock of his hair. Creeped her out."

"Nasty," Joe said, making a face.

Declan laughed. He hadn't had this much fun in far too long. In his past life, he could never have friends. Not real ones anyway. Anyone who tried to be his friend wanted something, wanting to use his power for their own desires. His family wasn't much for gathering, either. Both brothers were off waging one war or another in the name of his father, his sister thought everyone should just get along, and his mother had little patience for the interests of others. What he thought of friendships seemed superficial, little more than a show of dominance. This was...nice.

Cate paced in front of the mirror. "That leaves Ray at Nouveau and Jennifer and Maxine at Chopped."

Declan set his water bottle in front of him. "All right. Talk to me about how these three would take a client asking them out."

"Ray would love it," Anastasia said. "But he's not looking for anything serious."

Joe cocked an eyebrow at her. "How do you know that?"

Anastasia shrugged. She unfolded one leg to reach for more nuts. "We went out twice. He said he can't get serious about anyone until he finishes writing his book."

"Not that old thing." Maeve shook her head.

"A writer?" Declan asked.

"Watches too many of those true crime series. He wants to publish *Astoria: Murder and Mayhem.*"

"Is that the latest title? I thought it was Astoria: Death by Design."

"That was last month." Anastasia wedged her rolled-up mat under her side and propped herself up on one elbow. "To Ray, everything is murder. Heart attack? Nope, poisoned. Car accident? Brakes were cut. The only peaceful death in his book is going out in your sleep."

"Smothered. Or drugged," Joe said. Everyone turned to look at him. "What? Come on, you know it's happened."

Cate tapped the glass with a fingernail. "All right, so it's probably not Ray. If we've got it narrowed to Jennifer and Maxine, let's take a walk in their shoes..."

While the others debated, Declan stood up to stretch near the window. The sky turned purple with the waning light and the first planet winked into view.

Declan surveyed this new crew. Cate, directing an investigation into the personal lives of Astoria's hair stylists, Anastasia who scrutinized every detail, Joe and his fabulous, skin-tight athleisure wear, and Maeve buzzing around them all.

In his old life, everything wasn't all clouds and doves as so many assumed. He, too, had been wounded by betrayal, abandoned by those who claimed to adore him. Yet here, in this small yoga studio nestled on a darkened strip along a western coastline, Declan's heart warmed, aglow for the first time in something real, as tangible as the rubbery mat at his feet.

He loved every moment.

"Friends," Declan said, reveling over the taste of that word in his mouth. "Let's continue this debate over pizza. My treat?"

They'd packed Joe off with the bulk of the leftovers. He'd eaten an entire Hawaiian pie himself and was tickled at the prospect of seconds for breakfast. Maeve climbed into Anastasia's car for a lift, and Cate said she wanted to meet Jack on the pier. Declan caught Maeve and Joe exchanging a look at Cate's pronouncement, but they said nothing.

Declan returned alone to the Ram & Rose. Pizza slices—a new favorite food—went into the mini fridge, and he consulted his endless task list. Thanks to one too many soda refills, his inexperienced body was wide awake. If he must be up, he might as well work.

A ripple of red and blue lights flashed in the windows. Pounding echoed through the door. "Coming," called Declan. Irritation pinched at his shoulders as he crossed to the door. Outside stood a familiar officer, his face an oval moon in the streetlight. Declan pressed his lips together. "Can I help you?"

The officer lifted his chin to peer behind Declan. "Saw movement inside. Unusual for this hour."

"No one here but me." Declan crossed his arms.

Rooney's eyes narrowed slightly and his Adam's apple shifted. "You're sure?"

Declan made a show of looking around the otherwise empty room. "Yep, pretty sure. Do you check every business at night?"

Rooney bristled. "It's my job to keep tabs on things and assume anything could be suspicious."

Declan stepped forward into the threshold, as though to block the shop from further scrutiny. "Nothing suspicious here.

"That a fact?" A slow grin spread across Rooney's face. "Started packing yet?"

"No, why would I?"

Rooney rested his hands on his belt. "Jess didn't have any close relatives. House'll likely go up for auction. I doubt the new owners will want a random renter on their property."

"Too bad for them. I've paid for the year."

Rooney's eyes went wide. "You what?"

"Not that it's any of your business," Declan said.

"I wouldn't get too comfortable," the man said, glowering. "Folks get sloppy when they think they're off the hook."

"Why would I worry about something like that?" Declan had a few inches on the man and postured to take advantage of each one. "Unless I'm under some kind of investigation. Could that be why you stopped by tonight?"

Rooney shook his head. "Just doing my duty. Wouldn't want you to have to clean off more of those...bananas. Or worse." Rooney locked eyes with Declan.

"Is that a threat—officer?"

Rooney's nefarious smile was back. "Consider it a friendly warning." He tipped his hat and shuffled off, whistling.

TEN

"It's great," Maeve said. She turned the computer screen back to face him.

"Nearly there. Still short though." After their night at Slice Town, the group was no closer to sussing out the writer's identity. In a compromise, they'd blended what they knew of both stylists to craft a response. "Wouldn't have been able to do it without you."

"We want to help," Maeve said. "Intent is half the battle. Besides, your solution was brilliant."

Declan propped his chin in his hand, elbow on the bar. "Hoping we get another note. I could use a little more fodder."

"Patience," Maeve said. "A month from now, you'll be drowning in questions."

"How about customers, too, if I'm making a wishlist?"

The shop was empty. Declan had ample time to chalk out where he wanted Sturrock to build the shelves, alphabetize the plants, build a spreadsheet of his inventory, and spend far too long researching terrarium gravel.

Maeve pushed back from the bar and picked up her coffee

cup. "End of summer quiet, is all. My advice? Enjoy it. Get yourself together. Holiday season will be here before you know it. You'll scarcely have time to eat, let alone sleep."

Declan sat up from his slouch. "What about a promotion?"

"To see who has the saddest love life?"

"Not something I'd ever want to judge. I'm thinking more like a passport."

"Tell me more."

Declan sketched out a design on the back of his scone wrapping from Pastry House. "A stamp card. With boxes for each business that takes part. Visit all of them and the card is worth a discount at one of the shops. Something like that."

Maeve considered his drawing. "I like it," she said. "I could make mine a free class."

"And I could do a free plant." Declan had received a double shipment from his distributor. After an hour on hold, a Melanie in sales insisted Declan keep the plants for his troubles. Piles of spiky Tillandsia overflowed from within a bowl.

"Fisher at Seastar Resort would kick in. He owes me, anyway. Olafson at the fishmonger's. Archer at the bookshop, too. The more I think about it, the more people I know who'd want in."

"I bet Sophia would sign up." Declan held up the paper sack.

"Oh, she'll do it, all right, if I have to hogtie her to that oven."

"Seems like overkill."

"That old crone," Maeve said, and lifted her mug for emphasis, "has nothing better to do than speak ill of the dead. This would give her something to occupy her time and mouth."

"What?"

"She and Lisa. The two of them are no better than clucking hens."

"I don't know a Lisa."

"Owns Sand and Sea. Pretends she's a natural redhead."

"The place with the wind catchers in the window? Has those signs that say *Life's a Beach* and *Sand by Me*?"

Maeve nodded. "Cheap garbage she imports from overseas. That insufferable woman asked Sophia if she was enjoying the peace and quiet. Had a smirk wiped across her pointed little face and asked Sophia if she was interested in expansion. Didn't hear what Sophia said, but Lisa saw me and commented how it's a shame people don't get help when they need it."

Declan frowned. "What was that supposed to mean?"

Maeve shuffled to the door. "Seems some are spreading lies about Jess. That she didn't slip and fall from the widow's walk. Terrible name, come to think of it."

Declan remembered Jess's big plans. Her upcoming date and the wedding pitch with the scrumptious cinnamon rolls. Love for her family's home. She wouldn't have given up on the cusp of such a possibility. He tried to remember that night with Jess, the railing firm under his hands. The construction seemed safe enough, hadn't it?

"Maeve," Declan said. "What if it wasn't an accident?"

"I'm going to need another cup for this."

Declan pointed to the kitchen. "Help yourself."

From the kitchen, Maeve called to him. "What are you planning to do with this?"

Declan guessed what had caught her eye. He'd spent half the night before cleaning up an old machine. Stainless steel shone where grimy gray had been. "Not sure. If it works, I could sell it. Should fetch a decent price."

Maeve returned with a full cup. "I remember when Captain Rick used to run that thing on Saturdays. Kids would line up down the block in front of that door. He'd lean out over the top half and sell those sugar bombs until he ran out. Can't say I didn't snag a sack or two myself. Nothing better than a piping hot donut, fresh from the fryer."

"Maybe I should sell donuts instead of plants," Declan said.

"Or both? Plenty of folks have more than one business. Look at me, I'm one half yoga, one half healthy snack food store." She nodded to the case of coconut water on the counter she'd brought. "All right, now back to Jess."

Declan took a deep breath. "I didn't know Jess like you all knew her. I wish I had. But she didn't want to die."

"Agreed," Maeve said, reseating herself on a stool.

"I've been up on that roof. What if she was...pushed?"

The question sat there in the room with them, taking up space. Maeve broke the silence. "Don't think I haven't considered that—"

"And?"

Pax knocked at the half-open door and strolled in. He set a jar of jam on the counter. "From Mom," he said. "It's Salal."

"Sa-who?"

"It's a berry, grows in the woods. We pick a ton this time of year. Put one on your doorstep, too," he said to Maeve.

"How is your mom?" Maeve gave Pax a knowing look.

Pax shifted, uncomfortable. "Better," he said, and looked away.

Declan hoisted the dark berry concoction up to the light. "Whatever it is, it looks delicious."

"We pick the berries every summer," Pax said. "Have since Dad died. It was his favorite."

Declan glanced back to the kitchen. "I've got an idea. Who's up for taste testing?"

Within an hour, they had the first batch.

Pax shoveled one, then two more in his mouth. Maeve took a bite and closed her eyes in pleasure. "Fried dough is amazing. Can't believe I ate the forest equivalent of twigs and berries for far too many...well, much too long when something like this existed."

Declan bit into the soft circle, its golden brown outside streaked with a dark purple. *Magical.* He was now in possession of a bonafide mini-donut machine.

"Chocolate next," Pax requested.

Maeve pressed a hand to her stomach. "I shouldn't, but I will. If I gorge myself on them now, I'll use the resulting stomachache to scare me off in the future."

Declan plated the rest of the berry rounds and began on the chocolate. "The old bartender here might have been on to something. I wonder what other flavors I could make. Maybe I could figure out the local favorites."

"Salmon," said Pax, then shoved another donut in his mouth. "Beer. Coffee. Sadness."

"Hmmm... not sure about the others," Maeve said, "but I like the coffee suggestion. Maybe a sea salt caramel?"

"Pax, how about you take the rest of these to your mom? As a thank you for the jam."

"And tell her I'd like to see her again at the studio," Maeve added. Pax flashed two fingers their way and ducked out the door. Maeve kept her eyes on the boy as he left the shop. "Though I doubt she'll come."

"You know her?"

"Wasn't sure at first, but now...it's in the tilt of his brow, the thin lips, that single dimple. He looks just like her. She used to come to a flow class...until Robert died," Maeve said, before Declan could ask. "Tore that boy up something fierce. Evelyn remarried a real estate guy, a successful one, but she's been...different. As though a light went out."

Declan poured the new batter into the hopper. The rich, chocolate-y goo dropped into the hot oil in soft, circular plops. "I've been thinking about Jess."

"Me, too. I thought the kid would never leave."

"I like him," Declan said. He readied another plate for the newest creations.

"When he's not drawing big yellow *bananas* on your wall."

"His friends did it, but he apologized anyway. Got me a clean kitchen out of it."

"Might need new friends," Maeve said.

Declan held a pair of tongs, ready to snatch the first donuts off the conveyor. "Sounds like he's found some. He wants to join a group that meets up to do 'table-top role-play'—whatever that is. Told him I'd let him host a game night here so long as he cleans up. I get the feeling he's teetering between these two sets of friends."

"Teenagers. Better they hang out in a supervised spot rather than roam the streets."

"I've been thinking about that." Declan handed one of the hot chocolate donuts to Maeve. "How dangerous is Astoria at night?"

"You want to know if someone could have snuck in that night to hurt Jess."

Declan looked at the treats on the plate, a sour taste in his mouth. "I can't get past how crumpled she looked. Like a rag doll."

"What was she wearing?"

Declan blushed. "Night things."

"Like, *special* night things?" Maeve raised both eyebrows, giving her the look of a startled owl.

"You assume I know what my landlady wears to bed?"

"Well, you are—" Maeve began "—observant," she finished.

"What is that supposed to mean?"

Maeve shrugged. She selected another donut and took a bite.

"Her car didn't leave the driveway, of that I'm sure. It was part of why I went over after work. The day before, she'd claimed to be swamped. She had a contractor she was meeting down at her rented kitchen. Also, it rained that night, and the ground was damp. The car would have left tracks if she'd gone anywhere."

"So, we can presume—but can't confirm—that she died in the night. We have no reason to think she took her own life because of all the plans she'd made and her love for that house," Maeve said. "What do we need next?"

"A list of suspects," Declan said.

"Starting with the contractor," Maeve quipped.

"Where's Cate with the lipstick?"

Maeve waved a hand in dismissal. "That harpy. I had to scrub that mirror something fierce. She just wanted me to clean it so she could see herself better in the reflection."

"Paper, then," Declan said, and got up to rummage in the small office. While elbows deep in an old banker's box of office supplies, he heard the door open and Maeve's greeting. Declan returned with a notebook to find a woman eyeing the plate of donuts.

"I'll take a dozen," a woman said. She wore a coat the shade of hot mustard and clutched a shiny red purse. "And one of those plants with the pink and green leaves. Visiting my mother-in-law this weekend—have to bring something."

Maeve nodded at the woman as though she was well

aware, then turned to Declan. "Liv said she could smell those down the block."

"Sure could," Liv said. "Brought me back to the days of the old donut window. I'd get some before every meeting of the Fisherwives Society. The girls couldn't gossip half as long with their faces stuffed with sweetness."

Declan filled a sack with donuts. "On the house," he said. "I'm not in the donut business—yet. Thinking about it, though."

With Liv on her way to visit family, Maeve smiled. "Told you."

"I said I'd think about it," he said. "Now let's get back to the suspects." He proffered the notebook, promising himself he'd consider the donut side quest later.

"There are the usuals," Maeve said. She scribbled a few names on the list. "Petty thieves—"

"But nothing was taken."

"We don't know that for sure. What if it was something small?"

Declan crossed his arms. "Why would they have pushed her off the roof for something small?"

"Gold, diamonds, I don't know."

"Maybe it was going to be just a burglary, but things went wrong, and she caught the person. She would have been able to identify them."

Maeve nodded. "You could be right. Someone just wanted some antiques or something, but Jess woke up while they were there. Gar-bage ser-vi-ces," Maeve said, writing down the last two words.

"You think a garbage man killed her?"

"They're out early in the morning. They could have cased her house while everyone was sleeping."

Declan rolled his eyes. "You really think a garbage truck came to the house, collected the trash, then one of them thought it was a good idea to go into the house, up the stairs, and push the owner off a balcony?"

"Maybe she was out there already. The guy saw her and thought—"

"So, we're assuming it's a man?"

Maeve's eyes had darkened to a shade of violet. "I thought brainstorming was for considering all possibilities, not throwing each out. That's not very sporting of you, Declan."

Declan noted the roll consonants, a hint of a stifled accent when she pronounced his name. "I've never heard of a garbage man serial killer."

"Fine," Maeve said, through pursed lips. "So, who do you want to add?"

"What about an ex?" Declan asked.

"Hah. Not likely."

"Why not?"

"The man's a cop."

ELEVEN

Thunk. Thunk. A pounding at the door interrupted the brainstorm.

Declan swung open both halves to reveal a man wearing next to nothing in the chilly air. Over six feet tall, bronzed and glowing, he stood out against the dreary back-drop wearing the briefest of thongs. Water beaded off his skin and his golden ringlets maintained their bounce despite the drizzle. His eye color shifted from green to blue and back again. The man stood frozen on the step, holding a large red box tied with a sateen bow. A cream-colored envelope was tucked beneath the ribbon.

Maeve hopped off her stool to come to the door. "Well, invite him in," Maeve whispered over Declan's shoulder as she ogled the stranger.

"You're drooling on me," Declan said under his breath before addressing the man. "Can I help you?"

The man was reanimated as though a machine brought to life. "This is for you," he said, pressing the box into Declan's arms. "You are now the keeper. Take heed," he said, and winked in an over-exaggerated gesture. The man gave

Declan a short bow and resumed his stiff pose, muscles rippling up his arms and down the washboard of his stomach.

"Cool trick," Maeve said.

Declan assessed the man from head to toe, then looked at the box. "I should have known." He sighed and closed the door without further comment.

"Are you crazy? Some golden god was on your front step, and you don't even say goodbye? Let a gal at least catch his name." Maeve yanked the door open, but the man was gone. "Damn."

"Trust me," Declan said, appraising the box. "You're not his type."

"Not his..." Maeve stumbled over her response. "I'll have you know I've charmed entire armies, seduced royalty, brought anyone I pleased to my bed. Why, in my heyday..." Declan raised both eyebrows at her. "Metaphorically speaking. Well anyway, I would have at least liked to watch him leave."

"You have too many brain cells for the likes of him," Declan assured. He hefted the box. "Though one day I hope you'll tell me about all these conquests of yours. Sounds intriguing." He slid the envelope out from under the ribbon.

"Who's it from?"

Declan's expression darkened when he slit the envelope to reveal a cream-colored card. He scanned the message, sighed, and tossed it on the table toward Maeve.

Maeve picked up the discarded note and read while Declan untied the ribbon. "This is Lyncus. Don't listen to a word he says. Miss you. Love, Mom—*Mom*?"

Declan set his mouth in a grim line and lifted the lid.

A tuxedo cat poked its head up over the brim. It took in the shop in a wide-eyed assessment, then leapt from the box in one fluid motion. Alight on the bar, the cat stopped to clean its paws.

Maeve watched the creature, then turned to Declan. "Your mother sent you a cat."

"Not just any cat," Declan said, crossing his arms and regarding the new intruder.

Maeve looked from the cat to Declan. "What am I missing here?"

"Not sure yet," Declan said, glaring at the feline. "But when I find out, you can bet I'll blame my mother."

"Aren't you Mr. Handsome-Wandsome!"

This utterance came from Joe as Lyncus wound between his massive calves, rubbing his face across the man's hairless shins. The Bleeding Hearts had stopped by, alerted by Maeve of the new arrival.

"Who's a good kitty? Who's the bestest little kitty?" This was Maeve. She'd made it her duty to provide immediate victuals for the cat. Lyncus sniffed at the shred of shaved prosciutto she'd scrounged from the studio. He snagged it with his teeth in a delicate move before scarfing it at her feet.

"How could anyone not love such an angel?" Cate stooped to stroke the cat's spine.

Declan watched the proceedings, arms crossed.

"Yeah, Declan, tell us," Maeve said, one eyebrow arched.

"No gift from my mother is without its drawbacks."

"He's sweet," Cate said.

Declan shook his head. "Nothing from my mother is sweet. She hides the truth in false signs of affection, but I'm no fool. She is a master manipulator."

"You're right, this little guy is an absolute terror in disguise," Joe said, scratching underneath the cat's chin. His massive hand dwarfed the animal's face.

"So you have to feed a tiny animal. That doesn't seem too

hard." Anastasia offered Lyncus a saucer of milk. The cat purred upon receipt.

Joe made kissy sounds at Lyncus, and Declan considered, for the second time ever, if he needed to throw up. "What a well-behaved widdle man," Joe said. "Dressed up and everything. What's his name?"

"Lyncus," Declan said, and added, "He came with that name."

"Never heard that one before, but it suits," Joe said.

Declan appraised the cat. His friends were right, he was a good-looking cat. His white paws, white face patches, and the tip of white on his tail gave him the appearance of furry formal dress. "All right... Lyncus. Time to go home."

The cat shifted his gaze from his admirers to Declan and back, as though considering who he wanted for a master. In the end, he followed Declan, tail twitching with every step.

"There's a new card!" Cate held it aloft as though it were a prize torch.

"We're not set up yet," Anastasia said. "Almost." She'd shooed them out of the studio long enough to set up her preparations. While Maeve hung up the mats and shelved the blocks, Anastasia busied herself among the cushions. "I even brought placemats!"

Declan, Joe, and Cate trooped back into the studio.

"Ooooh," Joe said. "What's all this now?"

In front of each cushion was a steaming cup of tea. A larger teapot sat on a trivet. On a large wooden plank straddling two yoga blocks was a rainbow charcuterie spread. Anastasia beamed as they exclaimed over the craftsmanship.

"It's beautiful," Cate said.

Joe pressed her back. "Wait, I'm going to take a picture.

The paper could do a spread on these. Beautiful Charcuterie of the Port." He pulled out his phone from the pocket on his shorts and snapped several pictures from multiple angles.

"I've never seen anything like this," Declan said. He'd been at many feasts in his life, but none so lovingly prepared.

Anastasia rattled off the list. "There's banana chips and that's spicy soppressata. Pickled peppers, three kinds of olives, that killer honey lavender goat cheese, garlic hummus, chocolate-covered coffee beans..." She continued to point at and name each culinary delight. "The fancy Brie with that dehydrated strawberry powder sprinkled on top. Oh, and Joe's favorite—wasabi peas."

"You've outdone yourself, my dear," Maeve said, contributing a box of wine to the tableau. "Tell the kids to what we owe this bountiful celebration."

"I got a promotion!"

"Congrats!" Cate cheered. "I told you it was in the bag."

"Incredible as always," Joe said, and Anastasia blushed.

Declan hoisted his tea cup, "To Anastasia! What's the new title?"

"Operations Manager," she said. "I coordinate surveillance and any special projects."

"Special projects?" Joe sipped at his tea. "Mmm...jasmine, my favorite."

Anastasia smiled as she reached for a cracker coated on one side with sesame seeds. She topped it with a wedge of pear and a slice of prosciutto. "Depends on the customers. Still mostly land surveillance, but anyone with the funds can hire us."

"I'd like to see one of your drones sometime," Declan said. He spread smoked sturgeon on a bagel cracker and handed it to Cate before making a second for himself. Lyncus watched him, purring, until Declan slipped him a shred of fish.

"I love showing them off," Anastasia said. "Anytime."

Cate refilled her teacup from the pot, added wine to her

water bottle, and addressed the group. "Thank you all for coming, and much thanks to the fabulous Anastasia for bringing an incredible spread." She burped and covered her mouth. "Excuse me. Ahem. I hereby call this meeting of the Bleeding Hearts Club to order."

Maeve leaned over to Declan. "Give that woman an inch..."

Cate glared. "First, old news: Declan, how's the first submission?"

"It's good," Maeve said. "I've read it."

"I'm going to need more submissions to keep this up, though."

"Oh, don't you worry." Cate held up the card and waggled her eyebrows. She cleared her throat, took a sip of wine, then began. "The guy I like still has feelings for the woman that left him months ago. The other day, I caught him wearing a jacket she gave him—and nothing else. When we are out, everything is fine, but I can't help but think there's a ghost of a woman between us. What do I do?"

"Wow," Joe said. "How do you bounce back from that?"

Declan kicked back, ready to listen.

"I guess I'd want to know how long he was with this other woman," Anastasia said, serious despite the contents of the letter. "Some loves are harder to get over. Healing takes time."

"Jacket-wearing time, apparently," Declan quipped, and Maeve snorted.

Joe regarded Anastasia, gnawing at his lip. Declan watched him, curious about the way those two danced around each other.

Cate mused aloud. "I think I would want to know if this writer has insecurities that might turn something reasonable into something much bigger."

"Smart," Declan said. "They call jealousy the green-eyed monster for many reasons."

"What I never understand," Maeve began, "is why people never ask the questions they want answered."

Anastasia reached for an olive. "I think we want the answers but not the action that will have to follow. Or maybe that's just me." She looked at Declan and pointed to her empty ring finger. "Used to be a Mrs."

"I like the honesty card here," Cate said. She tucked a lock of hair behind her ear. "One year I hardly saw Jack, he was gone so much. Claimed he was fishing, but a wife knows."

Declan watched Maeve grimace at Joe who pressed his lips together.

Cate continued. "One day I followed him. He was down the coast at the next port. Found him feeding a stray pack of dogs outside the stewhouses."

"The what?" Joe sandwiched a slice of sausage between two crackers.

Anastasia muscled in her own question. "What did you do?"

"He saw me," Cate said, shrugging her shoulders. "Couldn't pretend I'd strolled by. So, we had it out. Then I let him get a dog."

"I'm all for that solution," Maeve said.

Cate shrugged. "I should have just asked him what was going on. Would have made things simple. Only made myself look bad."

"To honesty," Declan said, lifting his water bottle.

Cate tapped her bottle to his. "To the truth."

"This one was easy," Joe said, and palmed a half dozen lemon cookies from the tray. He looked at Declan. "Think you'll have another column?"

Declan nodded. "It's looking good."

Maeve scanned the circle. "All right, now that we've solved the town's love problems for the day, let's talk murder."

Anastasia's eyes went wide. "Murder?"

Maeve poured more wine into everyone's bottle and settled back onto her cushion. Declan said nothing, cringing on the inside.

"Declan and I want to know your opinions," Maeve said.

"It's not for the column," Declan added. "It's about Jess."

Anastasia bit her lip and looked away. Joe loaded up a pita chip, his mood somber.

Cate sniffed, then nodded to herself. "Makes sense. It's not like the cops are getting anywhere."

"You want to?" Declan thought the group would balk, call him and Maeve foolish for discussing the work of professional officers.

"Who better than a group dedicated to uncovering how the inner minds of the townspeople operate? We investigate love lives. Apply those same skills and there's no reason we can't catch a murderer." She brushed off her lap and dug into her purse.

"Wait!" Maeve stood up and crossed the room in bare feet. She dragged a large whiteboard from out of the closet, a couple markers in one hand. "Use this."

Cate uncapped the hot pink marker and wrote Jess in the middle of the board. "Most murders aren't random. They're done by someone the victim knows."

"How do you know this?" Anastasia regarded Cate with a wary eye.

"A girl picks things up when she spends enough time on the docks. Now, what are the motivations for murder?"

"Love, lust, loot, uh..." Joe counted them off on his fingers. "And loathing."

"Correct." Cate wrote these in the four corners.

Anastasia mouthed to Joe, "How do you know that?"

He shrugged.

Cate faced them again. "The question is, who would kill

our Jess? How about we frame our suspects through motivation."

"Only one problem," Joe said. "Everyone liked Jess."

Anastasia swept some cashews into her hand. "No one is universally liked," she said. "It's not possible."

"What do you say to that?" Light danced in Maeve's eyes as she questioned Declan.

Declan demurred. "It is a very human thing to want to be liked."

"We need to consider who wasn't Jess's biggest fan," Joe said.

Anastasia scoffed. "Not liking someone doesn't mean you murdered them."

"No, but it definitely makes you a suspect," Maeve added.

Joe yawned, a sound that edged on a roar. Everyone looked at him. "What? My neighbor's kid got a new drum set."

Anastasia winced. "Been there. I should get going, too." She stood to stretch. "New duties start tomorrow."

"But," said Cate, admiring her diagram. "We've hardly started in on our first investigation."

Declan consulted the diagram. "How about between now and the next time we meet, everyone comes up with a suspect and motive? I've got Sturrock coming early, and I need to sleep."

"Aye, aye, Captain."

Lyncus followed Declan home. At the apartment stairs, the cat bounded up the steps behind him, followed him inside, and curled up on the end of Declan's bed. The beast's green eyes followed Declan as he shrugged out of his jacket, set his notebook on the table, and microwaved a burrito. Declan grumbled through these tasks, stopping to narrow his eyes at the intruder. Lyncus was a handsome animal and thus far, hadn't caused any trouble. But if Declan knew anything about his mother, it was that she did little without reason.

Declan bagged up his trash and tucked his empty wine bottles under his arm as the cat watched, whiskers twitching. He lugged his garbage down the stairs to the cans at the side of the garage. When he lifted the can lid to deposit his bag, he noticed another bag waiting at the bottom.

"Ha," Declan said aloud. "Couldn't have been a garbage man. Wasn't even the right day." He lifted the lid off the blue recycling bin to add his bottles. On top were a dozen sheets of sketch paper, each of a towering wedding cake. Declan retrieved the top drawings and flipped through the collection. On most, a mermaid perched on one tier, flipping her tail over and down the side of the cake while a human groom in board shorts stood nearby. Shells and sea stars decorated the top and tier edges. Jess had written notes on the sketches, including measurements and a call for blue-green shimmer dust and edible pearls. In the margin, she'd written, *two flavors TBD, no chocolate, wheat allergy.*

Declan held Jess's ideas for the big wedding. If these draw-ings were any indication of the rest of her plan, she would have landed that contract. He selected one, the most complete of the drawings, and set the rest back in the bin. If the forensics team didn't take them, Declan felt no guilt over keeping one for himself, to remember her by. He closed the lid and tipped the can back to drag it to the curb.

On the ground below the can lay a familiar metal tube pressed into the gravel. Its ribbed, golden casing reflected light from the street lamp. Declan plucked it out from the dirt and tossed it into the trash bin. Jess would never have the chance to wear that shade again.

TWELVE

S unshine burst through the window, beaming down on Declan's face. A kneading pressure on his chest gave way to pinpricks of pain on his skin. He opened his eyes to find Lyncus on his chest, staring at him.

"What the—" Declan flailed. He attempted to sit up and tumbled half out of the bed. Lyncus dove for safety in a chair.

Declan rubbed at his eyes and shuffled to the sink. He picked up his phone to find a text from Maeve. "She hates to text," Declan told Lyncus. The cat hopped onto the counter as though to read.

Article on Jess. Dear Declan is out. Congrats.

Declan navigated to the *Astorian* online, then scrolled past his own article until he spotted the one on Jess.

Local woman who fell to her death from the third story of her family home had alcohol in her system. Neighbors and friends report that she'd been acting differently, and they were concerned for her well-being. There was no sign of forced entry at the residence.

"Ridiculous," Declan said to Lyncus. "She was busy." He kept reading.

> Investigations into the faulty railing on the widow's walk in the historic home are ongoing. Residents are urged to have their own structures inspected annually.

"Son of a siren!"

"Absolute trash," Declan boomed. He'd waited all of five seconds after entering the newspaper offices before laying into Joe. "How could you let them print this garbage?"

Joe grabbed Declan by the shoulder and ushered him away from the open newsroom. "Did you even read yours? I thought you were here to celebrate."

"I'll celebrate when there's justice!" Declan fumed.

"Shhhh," Joe said, scanning the sea of cubicles. Declan had marched straight to the offices of the *Astorian*, ready for battle. Joe nudged him farther down the hall. "Come into the break room. I heard they have cake."

Declan grumbled as he followed Joe through the office. Strips of wallpaper peeled off the yellowed walls. A florescent light buzzed overhead. In the small break room, little more than a converted janitorial closet, Joe turned to Declan. "You *have* to keep your voice down."

"I wasn't shouting, I was calm—"

"You brought Lyncus?"

Declan looked down at his feet. The cat waited as though in line for a coffee refill. "I didn't know he came in. Must have slipped through the door before it shut."

Joe squatted next to the cat. "Please keep out of sight, little man. Uncle Joe can't afford to get fired from this job, too, okay?" When Joe straightened, he towered over Declan. There was little space in the tiny room. "That cat deserves better than to be your afterthought."

Declan spotted the cake on the table. "Happy birthday Joe? I didn't know. Would have brought you a gift."

"Huh?" Joe followed Declan's gaze. "Oh, yeah. I had to give HR a date, you know how they are. I always forget until they remind me. It's lemon—if you like that kind of thing."

"I...don't know if I like lemon..." Declan said, frowning over Joe's statement. What did he mean about HR? He'd ponder that later. "Look, I thought the press was all about telling the truth. Why would they print something that made Jess look like a clumsy drunk?"

"Shhh," Joe hissed as a woman in a plaid skirt brushed in, humming to herself. Lyncus skittered under the small table to avoid the clip of her heels. Without a glance toward either man, she refilled her mug from the heated carafe and left. When the sound of her footsteps faded down the hall, Joe said, "First of all, I'm not the front page guy. I'm not in charge of any of that stuff. Second, relationships run deep in this place. You never know who is publishing what for whom. And last, did you ever consider that maybe there is something to the report? Many people hide their truth." He met Declan's eyes. "You said that yourself."

Undeterred, Declan tapped a finger against Joe's chest. "You know even better than I do that she wouldn't go out like that."

Joe put a steadying hand on Declan's shoulder. "You said yourself, she liked to watch the sunset up there. Maybe she had a little too much wine and it was a horrible, sickening accident."

Declan shook his head, emphatic. "There's no way. I didn't

hear her scream. Tipsy or not, you would make noise if you fell. And if she was too bombed to mind the railing, there's no way she would have made it up the stairs to begin with. They're little more than a glorified ladder."

"I do remember that," Joe said. "Used to mow her gran's lawn when I was a kid. Got to play with Jess sometimes and she'd sneak me up there."

Declan eyed the giant of a man, curious about what he was like as a younger person. "I didn't know you'd been friends that long."

Joe gave Declan a somber look. "She was one of the only people who never made fun of the way I looked. Her and Zelda."

"Then you know why this is eating me up. It just doesn't make sense. It rained that night, Joe. There was no sunset to watch."

Joe pressed his lips together, then stooped to pick up the cat at his feet. He stroked Lyncus's fur, thinking. "All right mate, I'll do some digging. But be careful what you say and to whom. I've got a lot on the line."

Declan spotted the new card before he unlocked the door to Ram & Rose. Maeve's studio was dark, the first class not until noon. He detached the crisp rectangle from the cork board and took it with him into his shop.

Lyncus trotted in behind Declan and took his morning inventory, as was his new routine. Declan found himself disappointed that thus far, no mouse nor errant moth dared show itself to the feline.

Declan set the card on the bar, then removed a piping hot ham and cheese croissant from his bag. He tore off a corner and offered it to Lyncus. The cat started forward, then hesitated.

"Come on, I don't hate you," Declan said. "It's not your fault my mother's using you as some kind of pawn." With another delicate sniff, the cat claimed the prize. "She is never without an ulterior motive. For all I know, she's outfitted you with a built-in camera behind one eye."

The cat looked up at Declan and blinked slowly, as though to demonstrate the harmlessness of his gaze. Satisfied with his snack, Lyncus sauntered over to his water dish.

Breakfast served, Declan picked up the card and read the scrawling text.

"If only I still had that power," Declan said to the anonymous writer, tapping the card against his palm. "Without that, you may be out of luck."

Declan wandered through the Astoria Sunday Market. Farmers laid out late summer crops, spreading their rainbow of produce out on the tables. Crafters hung their wares underneath the tents and stuffed them in bins. They crammed every inch of space with art that ranged from beautiful glass floats to watercolor paintings and hammered metal earrings. He purchased a pint of crimson tomatoes and a softball-sized watermelon. At the north end of the stalls, he ordered a burrito from a food truck and ate as he walked the rest of the way to the shop.

Lyncus gave the market a wide berth—too many dogs, Declan wagered—and met up with him on the pier. Declan walked as he ate, taking in the crowd, the gulls that begged for scraps, and the fresh air.

Ahead, Declan spotted Cate. Once again, she sat on the water side of the railing, legs dangling over the edge. He chewed quickly and hurried in her direction. The woman's back was to him, allowing the sun to highlight her multicolored locks. They shone like an underwater kelp forest, rippling below the waves. She wore some kind of green spandex, no doubt the latest in yoga attire.

A family approached the spot where Cate sat. Two parents snapped pictures as their toddler tried to catch a pigeon. Cate's head whipped their way. The child giggled and squealed each time a bird flapped just out of its reach.

Declan swallowed his bite. He opened his mouth to call out a greeting as the child tottered farther down the dock. Cate, her eyes on the family, dove forward off the pier. Her body arched in a practiced bow, her legs bound within her garment, its fabric shimmering like diamonds in the light, her hair streamers behind her curved form. Cate pierced the water's surface and was gone.

Declan stood, mouth open, for several heartbeats before rushing to the edge of the pier. He made it to the sturdy wooden railing at the same time as the child's mother.

"Did you see..." she said to Declan, her eyes on the water.

Declan could only nod, a slow confirmation. It had been Cate, he was certain of this. But where had she gone? The water rippled underneath the piers. Two ducks perched on a tumble of pilings, the fallen tree trunks moss-coated and slick. A cormorant landed on the remnants of an old dock and stretched its wings to dry in the weak sun. Both Declan and the woman stared into the water, willing the long-haired swimmer to surface.

"It's like she disappeared," the woman said. "Should we call someone?"

"We could," Declan said, "but what would we say?"

The woman smiled, her eyes sparkling. "They tell you to never turn your back on the water. I assumed that was for safety. Now I know it's for wonder, too."

The man caught up to them, the squirming child in his arms, whining for freedom.

"What are you all looking at?" the man asked, his voice affable. The crown of his hat displayed an emblem of waves with *Landlubber* embroidered beneath.

"A fish," the woman said, and winked at Declan.

THIRTEEN

"I call this meeting of the Bleeding Hearts Club to order," Cate said. She tapped a breadstick on the side of her water bottle. "This is a special meeting dedicated to the investigation into the death of Jessica Black. May we take a moment of silence to think of our departed friend."

Cate bowed her head. Declan didn't close his eyes like the others. Instead, he watched Cate. He was certain it had been her by the docks. She tossed her long hair over her shoulder, took a deep breath in, and released it. "All right. So, what have we got?"

"Random," Maeve said. "A burglary gone wrong."

Declan rolled his eyes. "Not the garbage man theory again."

"It could have happened!" Maeve swirled her breadstick in a cup of crimson marinara. "The truck came by, the guy thought he'd sneak into a fancy old house and snatch something. She was up early like a lot of chefs, surprised him, and he had to make sure there were no witnesses."

Maeve set her marinara next to her knee where Lyncus attempted to dip a paw in the cup. Declan batted him away.

Lyncus moved to sit on an unopened pizza box, purring from the warmth.

Anastasia frowned. "A burglar did what now?"

"Maeve thinks the garbage man did it."

Maeve threw a foam block at Declan who ducked.

"Interesting," Cate said, reviewing the board. "What motivation do we think the garbage man had?"

"None," Declan said. "At least not this week. Garbage wasn't running down our street the night she was killed."

"All right, next—Joe?"

"Accident."

"No way," Maeve said. "You think she just fell?"

"Writing it down," Cate said.

Joe shrugged. "I don't know. Been overhearing reports that she'd had a lot to drink that night." Joe seemed to catch the fire in Maeve's eyes and doubled back. "I don't think she meant to —I just think it happened."

"My turn," Anastasia said. "What if it was... Sophia?"

Everyone else chimed in. "What!?"

Joe frowned. "The baker?"

Cate reached for another breadstick and dipped it into her cup of cocktail sauce. Declan had ordered pizza in so they could meet in the seclusion of Mudra. When Cate had pulled the unexpected condiment from her purse, he'd blinked at her choice but said nothing.

"But she's so sweet," Cate said of the elder baker. "Literally."

Anastasia cracked open the container of pesto. "Phoebe said Sophia came in to ask about the ownership of Jess's half of the building. The woman's barely been gone a week, and she's moving in!" She turned to Declan. "Phoebs works in the county offices. Says she sees paperwork in her sleep at this point."

Declan nodded. He thought back to the day of construction, the way Sophia ground her teeth over the situation with Jess, and the conversation Maeve overheard in the pastry shop.

"What about you?"

All eyes turned to Declan. He'd mulled the question over and over since the day he saw Jess's body in the bushes, but he couldn't make the pieces fit. "Could be the new guy she was dating... or about to date. Maybe he came on too strong."

"I didn't know she was dating again," Cate said, lifting her eyebrows. "That was a quick rebound."

Declan opened his mouth to explain the calendar appointment, but Joe jumped in. "Who do *you* think it is?"

"A ghost," said Cate.

"No." Maeve crinkled her forehead in disbelief. "On what plane of existence does that make sense?"

Cate shrugged. "You know those old places are haunted. It's why most of them are rentals. People make big bucks off tourists who want to scare themselves for a night. I doubt her grandmother was the only person to die there. What if the spirit of someone else wanted her gone?"

Anastasia shook her head. "That's ridiculous."

"Says the woman who accused the little old pastry chef," Cate snapped back. She put her hands on her hips. Declan spotted a tattoo of a wedding band around her ring finger.

"We may have a way to go before we're ready to throw out accusations," Maeve said. "I vote we table the discussion until after Jess's funeral. We need more suspects. That and the pizza's getting cold."

Declan locked up his shop after his friends—people who were kind to him without any coercion, people who liked him in this imperfect form—left. Even Lyncus chose his allegiance to some degree. Declan hadn't leashed the cat, let alone picked him up, since his arrival.

As Declan trudged up the hill, a potted catnip in one hand, the cat in question trailing behind, he mulled the night's discussion. The Bleeding Hearts had shifted from the impossibility of anyone going after Jess to everyone from the garbage man to an unknown specter. They were getting nowhere, and the case was growing cold.

The house loomed ahead. Declan paused in the driveway to take in its mass. The beautiful Victorian lay vacant, and in that darkness, foreboding.

Declan headed for his stairs when from inside the house came a crash.

There were no lights on inside and the curtains didn't stir. Declan scanned the yard, but the only movement came from a dripping gutter, overflowing with leaves. Declan skirted the side of the house and approached the back. The door was open. Declan approached the door, Lyncus on his heels. Inside, the house was silent.

"Stick close," he whispered to the cat. "I don't want you scaring me."

The porch steps squeaked under his weight. Inside the kitchen, he stopped to call out. "Hello?"

There was no answer.

Declan took one step and then another, each floorboard protesting his entry. The house was dim. A fine layer of dust lay on the furniture, the countertops, and floor.

In a flash of movement, Lyncus jetted past Declan. He launched himself over the back of the couch. There was a tussle, a screech, and two furry brown shapes shot past Declan and out the back door, Lyncus on their tails.

"What in the?" Declan tripped over a footstool and fell back into the music cabinet. He righted himself, then hurried after the chase.

In the yard, two raccoons faced one furious feline. To his credit, the cat made an impressive stand, back arched, hair standing straight up. Lyncus meowed, hissed, and spat at the intruders. Declan reached for a shovel leaning against a fence and waved it at the raccoons. The pair scampered off into the night, their masked faces turning back to ensure they weren't followed.

Relieved, Declan let out the breath he'd held. "I think they're gone," he said to Lyncus. "Let's close up and get to bed."

Declan took the back porch steps two at a time. When he reached around to lock the knob from the inside, he heard the faint tenor of Pavarotti from the living room. He closed the door with a soft click.

Perhaps the house was home to something, still.

"This might be my favorite flavor."

"Which one?"

"Chai, all the way."

"Any you don't like?"

Pax chewed and swallowed. "Pumpkin. It's overdone. Save it for a holiday special."

"I've got to make it through my first health inspection before I can even think about specials," Declan said. There'd been no walk-in customers that day, but two people had called for flower arrangements.

"I'm sorry, I don't carry any," he said for the second time that afternoon. "Of course I will consider it...Yes, thank you." Declan hung up the call. "Apollo's hole," he muttered.

"I like that one," Pax said. "Can I use it?"

"Can you use—oh. Sure, but don't tell him where you got it. Or your mom, okay?"

"Of course," Pax said. "But why don't you?"

"Why don't I what?"

Lyncus hopped into Pax's lap, kneaded his thighs for a moment, then settled. Pax stroked the cat's fur. "Carry flowers. You've got all these plants which are nice and all, but they're more...permanent. Some people are looking for something temporary."

Declan picked up a bushy fern. He rotated the pot, checking the soil for moisture with his thumb. "What do you mean?"

"Mom says it's like makeup versus a tattoo. You wash makeup off every night, so you get to enjoy lots of colors, but a tattoo is sticking around."

"I think I get it," Declan said. "I guess I'm just tired of... flowers. Roses in particular. No one has any originality anymore. Get sick? Yellow roses. Someone dies, they get white. Break a heart? Send pink with a little stuffed bear." Declan made a gagging motion.

Pax ran his hand from Lyncus's forehead to his tail. The cat stretched his spine in response. "But this place is named—"

"My sister's idea of a joke," Declan said, lips pressed into a line.

"It's your shop, I guess. But if you're going to make money..." Pax looked around at the empty shop. "My stepdad loads my mom with a bouquet from the grocery store every other week. I'm sure she'd be happier if he got them from you."

"What does he get her?" Declan filled his watering device at the sink.

"Red roses, mostly."

Declan groaned. "See!"

"You know," Pax said, lifting Lyncus from this lap. The cat clung to the boy's denim with Velcro claws. "For someone who's generally nice, you've sure got a bitter side." Claws free, Pax set Lyncus down on the small bed Joe had dropped off that morning on his way to the paper. "When was the last time someone sent you roses?"

Pax's question flattened Declan like a tornado through a cornfield. "I...don't know that anyone ever has." Memories he'd worked hard to stuff away surfaced, bringing with them that familiar ache. He thought of the past, thought of *her*. Declan snapped his eyes shut, willing inner calm to return. When he was certain he was breathing again, he opened his eyes to face the teen.

"Let's just say that at my age, roses for me are like ice cream to a kid working at a creamery. Day after day scooping cones burns you out on Rocky Road."

"Dunno," Pax said as he grabbed his skateboard from its resting spot near the door. "Maybe you just need a different flavor."

With Pax gone, Declan stewed. He'd scrubbed every inch of the kitchen, rearranged the hanging plants by size, and started categorizing the succulents by color when the phone rang again, disrupting his inner monologue.

"Hello? No, I'm sorry, we don't carry cut flowers—yet. But I've been thinking about it. There've been so many requests today that I—oh. *Oh.* I'm so sorry, I should have known. I wish I could help. She was a wonderful woman. I understand...I will. Thank you, take care."

Declan ended the call, pressing the phone against his chest. Lyncus stared at him from his perch on the bar, the cat's peridot eyes aglow. "I'm a complete idiot," he told the cat. "Good thing you appear to own a suit."

FOURTEEN

Declan covered the basket of donuts with a cloth napkin. He'd never attended a funeral, so the preparations were another first. In *Southern Heartache,* he'd read about the casserole requirement for all memorial services. But five minutes on the internet and Declan was lost in a sea of possibilities without a full kitchen. Donuts he could manage.

Anastasia picked him up in her compact electric car. He sat at an angle to give his knees space in the cramped passenger seat. He clutched at the basket, numb.

"You look nice," Anastasia said, in assurance.

He'd worn his one suit, a navy so dark one had to squint to tell it from black. Declan tugged at the ends of his sleeves, his cufflinks gold anchors against the fabric. "So do you," he said.

Anastasia wore a black dress printed with big pink peonies. "Thank you. They're Jess's favorite. You'll get to see them in bloom next spring," she added, her eyes on the road.

Declan stared out the window as the town rolled by, not bothering to mention he wouldn't be there much past next spring. They passed the library and the maritime museum, continuing down the highway. At the gas station, people stood at the pumps as oil glugged into their gas tanks. A bicyclist raced by in orange and blue spandex. Astorians carrying on with life while he and his friends mourned a death.

The service was brief. A priest made grand statements about a simple woman who'd dared to want more, to turn a dream into reality. Taken too soon. May she rest in eternal peace. Declan memorized the art on the chapel walls, the hairstyles of the people in the rows in front of him, and counted backward from three hundred. Twice. He avoided the large, satin-draped coffin at the front of the room and wouldn't allow himself to focus on the blown-up photograph of Jess, head tipped back in laughter, on a giant easel ringed with white roses. In an idle thought, he wondered where they got the flowers.

After the crowd had their chance to weep over the remains of their friend, they shuffled out onto the cemetery grounds for the burial. Again, the insipid priest contributed little, and a cousin of Jess's no one seemed to recognize tossed in the first handful of dirt.

Declan scanned the gathered crowd for signs of glee, malice, or unusual interest. People stood, hands clasped, talking softly, or sniffling into tissues. There were faces he recognized and many he didn't. Would a murderer come to the funeral of their victim?

When the priest began his solemn walk back to a waiting car, Declan wandered among the headstones while Anastasia chatted quietly with other attendees. Declan skirted the crowd, reading inscriptions for pioneers, congressmen, children, and beloved mothers.

From behind the hemlock, its tiny pinecones littering the ground, a flash of purple caught Declan's eye. He ducked around an azalea and spotted a familiar round silhouette making her way between the graves. Declan followed, staying back behind the trunks.

At a large marble headstone carved with a massive rose, the woman knelt to set a bouquet on the site. Declan crept closer until the woman was a few paces away. She set her hand on the marble a moment before pushing herself back up to her feet.

"I'm sorry, Zelda. I know I let you and her daddy down. Kept an eye out as best I could. Though she drove me batty with all her ideas. It wasn't even the hammering and pounding so much as the flitting about, never settling down. She wanted so much, Zee. In the end, I wasn't there to help her get it."

"It wasn't her," Declan said.

Maeve sat on a round purple cushion. She attacked the pieces of a shelving unit with a screwdriver and a set of faulty directions. "How do you know?"

"She sounded too...defeated." Declan confessed to eavesdropping on Sophia's graveside confession.

"But did she say she didn't do it?"

Declan frowned. "Not exactly..."

"Then it's still possible."

Perched on his own cushion, Declan drew his legs up to his chest. He hunched forward, resting his chin on his knees. "So, I'm not allowed to use my instincts?"

Maeve ceased her twists of the screwdriver and peered at Declan. She raised one eyebrow. "You sure you have some... instincts?"

The unasked hid in Maeve's question. Declan picked at a loose thread on the edge of the pillow. "I used to. Hell, I was known for it at one point..." He trailed off. How could he explain his past to anyone, let alone a yoga studio owner in a random port town? He sighed. "I suppose we can't rule her out entirely, but can I at least be given a ninety percent likelihood she's innocent?"

"Granted," Maeve said. "But that means we're back to the garbage man."

Declan groaned. "Enough with that. The poor guy doesn't deserve this kind of harassment."

Maeve stood up, collecting the instructions and her tools. "Looks like a shelf to me."

"I never could figure out those hieroglyphics. All pictures, no words."

Maeve folded the paper in half. "Too often we use words to dig ourselves out of experience," she said, "when what we need to do is step in and get our hands dirty. See what matches, which pieces line up. Live first, explain and label later. There's talking about accomplishments, and there's getting things done." She held out a hand to the new shelf. "This is called getting it done."

Declan mopped his forehead with a face towel. "The next time you challenge me to attend anything with the word 'power' in it, I'm going to remember the deep-seated regret of this moment."

Maeve bent down to hand him his favorite coconut water. "I'm a motivational speaker. What can I say?"

When Maeve invited him to a new class, Declan was pumped at the opportunity. Now he lay flat on his mat, waiting for his heart rate to settle. "You know that savasana pose?" he said from the floor. "Which class lets me stay like that the whole time?"

"You have to get up sometime," Maeve said, padding past him to put away the foam rollers. "The others are on their way."

"I'm here early," Anastasia called from the door. She entered, a sheaf of papers in her hand. Her jacket was damp from outside. Spotting Declan on the floor, a sweat stain on the chest of his tank top, she said, "Power yoga?"

"How did you guess?"

"There's a reason none of us were here."

Maeve scowled. "Hey, this class is awesome."

Anastasia busied herself in sliding a few cushions toward Declan. "For people made of rubber, yes."

Maeve rolled her eyes. "So it's a little intense."

"Couldn't eat for half a day. I was so sore," Anastasia whispered loudly to Declan.

Joe shouldered his way into the room. "Need me to carry you someplace?" Joe set down a battered messenger bag to assess Declan.

"Thanks, but not yet. I kind of like the gelatinous experience."

"I'm telling you," Maeve said, taking a seat on a cushion, "you crave it after a tick."

Cate joined them from the reception area. "Why the emergency meeting? We don't go to power yoga."

"I called it," Anastasia said. "I have some new information. But first, what's the status of Declan's latest article?"

"It's a go," Joe said. They'd saved the new cards in the hopes Joe's boss would approve a weekly spot. "We had a few people write in about how much they loved the first one."

"Good. Any other old news?"

"Declan is all but certain it wasn't Sophia," Maeve said, adding, "and I agree. She didn't like Jess, may have resented her and hated the remodel, but she didn't want her dead."

Joe slid the white board out from between the cabinets. He ran a finger through the middle of Sophia's name. "Okay, what else?"

"I've been thinking," Cate said, her face drawn. "What if Jess took her own life?"

Maeve interrupted. She held her hand up to stop Cate's next words. "There's no way—"

"Hear me out," Cate said. "I know what it is to be on your own. She was alone in that house after a big breakup with no family. Her career was stalled. She may have been extra vulnerable. Being human is hard."

Declan cocked his chin at Cate's last comment. The mystery of Jessica aside, he'd come to the same conclusion. Dealing with the ins and outs of a short life span was no joke.

Joe stared at a spot in the center of their circle, thoughtful. "You're not wrong," he said. "We can't rule it out—the police haven't."

The mood in the group darkened. "You have news?" Maeve probed Anastasia.

"I do," Anastasia said. She flipped through the notes she carried before selecting a page. She cleared her throat. "From my niece, Phoebe."

Maeve leaned over to whisper to Declan. "Works at City Hall, nice girl. You two should meet."

"Several interesting records requests came across her desk this week. One Steve Corey wanted the details on Jess's house and a few other properties, as well as information on the owners, themselves."

"That was fast," Cate said. "She's barely in the ground and the sharks are circling."

"Wait"—Joe lifted a finger, brows drawn together—"Steve Corey, the real estate agent?"

Anastasia nodded. "Why do you ask?"

Joe shrugged. "Police just found his body floating under a pier. It'll be in tomorrow's paper."

"Wait—what?"

"Yep, Harvey covered the story. Was writing it up when I left."

Anastasia deflated. "Phoebe will be so disappointed. She was excited to help."

Cate patted her on the back. "Tell Phoebe she's welcome to join us anytime she can get away—and to keep an eye out. If there was one inquiry, there'll be more."

Joe looked down at the board. "We need more suspects."

FIFTEEN

Declan came home to a blown breaker—or so he'd diagnosed the darkness in his apartment with a little help from an internet search and a video channel called *Rebecca's Repairs*. According to Rebecca, he needed to find the electrical box. He stepped to the little window in his apartment. Other neighborhood lights were on, narrowing the source to a panel in the garage or the house. Rebecca said that older houses could be tricky and warned everyone to take care.

"Stay put," he said to Lyncus, who meowed in the dim glow from Declan's phone screen. The cat alighted on the bed and curled himself up to wait.

A frigid drizzle pelted Declan as he crossed the yard, looking over his shoulder. He'd already tried the garage door to no avail, its shiny new lock mocking his attempts. It was silly to hide, he told himself, he'd paid rent to be there. Still, he figured the less attention he brought to himself, the longer his new little world would remain untouched. There was hope that inside the house he would either find the source for the outage or a key to the garage.

Declan fumbled with his own key at the back door, dropping it between the porch boards. *So much for that hope.* A furtive search with the aid of his phone was no help. He rummaged in the drawers back in his apartment but found only a straightened paperclip and a butter knife, neither of which had any effect on the back door, and he quickly vetoed any attempts at the front door, facing the street. He rested his forehead against the door. Rain pelted his back in a soft staccato.

He could manage in a dark apartment overnight. An electrician could be found in the morning—but what would he say? Was he even allowed to have someone fix things at the house? Doing so would bring attention to him, too, as a tenant in a house owned by a dead woman, and there was little good in that.

Declan sighed and lifted his head, spotting a ladder leaning against the house. It stretched to the base of a second-story window, a yard debris bin at its base. He scaled the ladder one rung at a time, not trusting the soles of his shoes on the slippery metal. Near the top, he was in line with the gutters. On one side of the ladder, they were empty of leaves and muck. The other held a brown sludge, yet to be cleaned.

"What's this?" Declan poked at a patch of rubbery green material until it revealed first one finger and then another. He unearthed a single glove from the leafy muck. It was slim, much too small for him. Evidence of a chore Jess would never finish. He chucked the glove on top of the bin where it wouldn't clog the gutters and addressed the window.

Declan peered through the murky glass. The interior of the house was dark. Behind him, empty streets met in silence, sidewalks bare. He scoped out the window frame. Paint peeled in delicate stripes where the sash met the apron. The casing warped near one corner, a consequence of age and the rainy climate. There was a smear of filth near the latch and the glass was grimy. He doubted Jess bothered to scrub these windows, given their height. He pressed up on the sash, but it didn't give. After another check of the street, he wedged the butter knife between the sash and the sill. Declan pressed on the makeshift lever, and the window creaked, sliding open a crack.

Rain pattered against Declan's jacket as he wrapped his fingers around the bottom of the window and lifted. The window groaned open. He pushed the curtain aside and stuck his head through the opening.

Darkness, nothing more. With a heave, he was through. An awkward half somersault and he was upright again.

The room was sparse, a tidy bedroom with a single bed, a wardrobe, and a side table on which sat a lamp with a glass shade. Declan fumbled beneath the glass for the pull chain. When his fingers found the string of metal balls he yanked. Nothing.

"Well, that answers that."

Declan took a step and the floor creaked. He paused. The flutter of the curtain over the now open window was the only movement. Phone out again, Declan lit the path to the door and stepped forward, ignoring the floorboards beneath his feet.

The house had the stale scent of unmoving air, confined for far too long. As he padded down the steps to the first floor, the memory of his last visit with Jess sifted back through his mind. The beautiful home, a relic of a prosperous time, treasured by the family. The row of photographs marched by on his left as he descended, the entryway spilling open before him

He crossed to the kitchen first. A notebook lay open on the counter. It held more sketches of the mermaid cake and a list of ingredients. In the corner of the page was a gratitude list:

My hands to bake with.
Two feet to follow my dreams.
A steady heart to guide me.

Chocolate.

Gran's house to keep me warm.

This wasn't the list of someone who wanted to die.

There were sets of keys on a hook by the door. Each had a little tag with Jess's handwriting on the labels. One was marked *Garage* and Declan unhooked the ring. He almost missed the rectangular white card peeking out from under Jess's notebook.

"Steve Corey, real estate agent." Declan flipped the card over to find Friday's date scrawled on the back with a second phone number.

A scuffle from upstairs drew Declan's attention away from the book. "Is that you, Gran?" But there was no reply.

Ten minutes in the basement with Rebecca, and Declan had the breakers sorted. He took the steps up to the first floor two at a time and crossed to the living room, its high ceiling ringed with crown molding. With deft fingers, he selected an album from a vintage collection, flipped a switch on the record player, and lifted the needle into place.

"Enjoy," he said to anyone listening and left, *Pagliacci* playing behind him.

Wind whipped at Declan's hair. Lyncus perched two feet on Declan's shoulder with his hindquarters nestled atop the abandoned yellow tracksuit in the backpack. Declan was surprised when Lyncus cooperated with the arrangement. Together, they'd climbed the steep hill and up the many steps to the top of the Astoria Column. This landmark promised an experience worth the height, and Declan needed a new perspective.

From this vantage point, with a large tuxedo cat draped around his neck, Declan took in the three hundred and sixty-degree view. There was the mouth of the Columbia River, one of the most dangerous passageways in the world. The four-mile-long bridge from Oregon to Washington. A slew of barges, lined up and anchored, awaiting their orders. Houses flowed over the hillside and down toward Youngs Bay.

A man and a child stood at the rail, assembling a balsa wood airplane. Once it was air worthy, Declan watched the little girl launch the aircraft outward. It sailed over the small field and disappeared over the tops of the conifers.

Declan pressed himself up against the railing and stared downward. The ground waited over twelve stories below. He thought of Jess and the fear one would experience in a free fall. A woman on his right noticed him shiver.

"You okay?" She had soft brown eyes and a smattering of freckles across her cheeks. "You don't have to look, you know."

'Yeah, I know. Just thinking about...physics."

"Your cat's adorable," she said, holding her hand out to Lyncus. He sniffed her fingers, and she scratched under his chin.

"Don't tell him that. I can barely keep his ego in check as is."

The woman set her hand on his bicep and squeezed. "Hold the railing on your way down. Things can get a little woozy on the descent."

SIXTEEN

Declan woke to a sharp compression of his lungs. He blinked his eyes open, a rapid adjustment to the darkness within his tiny studio. He was in the habit of sleeping with the window cracked, no matter the weather, and he inhaled cool, moist air. Above him, a furry face loomed.

"Lyncus—what in all Hells!" The cat bumped his head against his owner in a repeated motion. "I was sleeping," Declan said, shoving the cat's head to the slide. He'd been dreaming—another novel sensation—that he captained a boat named the *Pythia*. Billowing clouds gathered on the horizon as shimmering dolphins swam alongside his vessel. Declan attempted to piece together the identity of a ship on the horizon, yet the spyglass fogged again and again. He wiped the glass clean only to find it in need of service. The ship drew closer, bearing down on Declan. Lyncus woke him in the middle of his manic swipe as the flag of his pursuer flapped into view.

The cat jumped down from the bed and padded to the door. He stood on his hind legs and brushed his front paws against the wood surface. On all fours again, he let out a throaty meow.

"What has gotten into you?" Declan swung his feet over the side of the bed and felt for his slippers. He mashed his fingers against the front of his phone with his hand to check the time. The screen glowed from its spot on the table. "Gods, it's two a.m. Did you have bad tuna or something?"

Lyncus repeated his desperate door scratching. From outside, there was the sound of glass clinking, followed by a crash.

Declan groaned. "Not again." He shuffled to the window and shoved the curtains aside. Rain splattered through the screen, and the sill was wet. He squinted at the yard through the downpour. Lyncus joined him, resting his front paws next to Declan's hands.

A shape manifested near the wall. Small and brown, it skittered across the yard. Two more followed. Darker patches of fur contrasted with light as they scampered off. On the ground near the garage, Declan picked out the overturned recycling bin, the blue container spilling contents over the lawn.

"Raccoons," he said to Lyncus. "Nothing more. Now be a good kitty and use your litter box. Neither of us should go out in this. You and I would both be washed into the river." Declan closed the window and crawled back under the sheets. He yawned, rolled over, and was asleep.

Lyncus remained by the window, green eyes flashing in the night.

Declan stepped one foot out the door into the open air. His hands flew out to grab the doorjamb before his body followed his footstep. His knee slammed down as he sat, hard, in the doorway. Declan willed his heart to slow its incessant pounding as one leg dangled out the door. Below him, the remnants of the garage stairs lay across the doorway, wood splintered. Declan stared at the debris, attempting to make sense of his predicament.

When he could trust himself to move again, he scooted backward into the safety of his apartment. He nudged the door closed with his recovered foot and withdrew his phone from his pocket.

"Y'ello," boomed Joe. "Don't tell me something juicy came up? Tell me one of those old biddies from the senior yoga wants advice on a threesome. That Shelly's a randy one, always winks at me."

"No. I mean, I don't know. I haven't been to the shop yet. Look, can you...come over?"

Ten minutes later, Joe looked up at Declan and Lyncus peering out over the door ledge. Joe's standing reach was just shy of the door. The giant of a man looked from the smashed stairs up to his friends. "You could jump," he suggested. "Fairly sure I could catch the both of you."

Declan didn't doubt the man, yet there was something undignified in that solution. "No need, but thanks. There's a ladder on the side of the house that should work."

Joe returned with the ladder over his shoulder, one beefy arm wrapped around the metal. He wrestled it into the soft earth and tilted the top against the wall. Joe set a foot on the lowest rung, anchoring the ladder in place.

Declan donned his backpack and crouched down. He pointed to the opening. "This is your ride," he said to Lyncus. The cat jumped into the bag and meowed in confirmation.

At the doorway, Declan took a deep breath to steady himself. He descended the ladder, one step at a time, grateful for the bulk of Joe ensuring their safety.

"Well," Declan said, after planting both feet on solid ground. "Got any ideas?"

"I might know a gal," Joe said.

Anastasia assessed the damage. Hands on her hips, she stared first at the pieces of the stairs and then at the side of the garage.

"What's the verdict, doc?" Declan, Joe, and Lyncus, still in the backpack, watched her assessment. She hunched down to paw the sandy dirt near the wall of the garage.

When she stood, she held up a nail. "Yanked out from the stringer."

"I take it that's bad," Declan said.

Anastasia pointed to a jagged-edged, large piece of wood splintered in two. "That is the stringer. Its job is to anchor the stairs, along with these galvanized nails. The problem you have is that the nails, or most of them, anyway, came out of the stringer. The stringer fell and took the stairs with it."

"I see," Declan said, though he didn't. Back home, his family thought little of skills like carpentry and sewing. Declan was learning these abilities were far more formidable than he'd been led to believe.

"The thing I don't get is the sudden collapse," Anastasia said, scratching her head. "I have a hard time accepting they all fell out all at once."

"These have seen better days." Joe kicked at the wood, sending a rail flying.

"Maybe," Anastasia said. "But"—she bent down to point at the holes on the stringer—"if they'd become worn over time, I'd expect the holes here and those in the house's side to be bigger. Like the nails strained against the wood over time." She crossed back to the wall. "These holes are fine. And also, check out the nails." Anastasia held the nails out flat in her palm. Each was angled, bent and misshapen.

Joe clapped Declan on the back. "Guessing you weren't out here attempting a home improvement project."

"I don't even own a hammer." Declan ran his hand through his hair. Here was a catastrophe that required minor construction and a reassessment of his personal safety. He reached back to stroke the top of Lyncus's head, grateful for his furry friend. "This day already requires a gallon of coffee."

"That problem, I can solve," Joe said.

They trooped down the hill to the Pastry House. Declan zipped up the backpack as they entered the shop.

A line of customers waited between the door and the counter. Sophia, flustered, buzzed around the espresso machine, steam billowing up from her efforts. They joined the line.

Declan unzipped a small section of the backpack so Lyncus could people watch.

"I don't suppose you know a quiet way to rebuild an outdoor flight of stairs?"

Anastasia shook her head. "I'm afraid not. That's a complete rebuild. No amount of glue will put that pile of toothpicks back together. Why are you worried about the noise?"

"I don't want to call attention to the fact that I still live there."

"Phoebe checked. Rental law says you're safe until the end of your lease. No matter what happens with the house."

Declan looked away, not wanting to reveal the worry he knew etched his face. He couldn't tell Anastasia that any kind of exposure, even a legal battle he'd win, was too big a risk. Anything that encouraged people to look into this past would cause problems. He stood on tiptoes to see over the crowd. Sophia pressed the back of one hand to her forehead, scribbling notes on a pad as the customer in front of her ordered a slew of drinks. "Everyone's out for lattes this morning," he said. "Must have been a late night."

While they waited, Joe checked his work email. "Got some stuff on Corey. The boys came through. Seems he'd been struggling—until recently. Was the purchasing agent for five properties in the last three months. Sold them before they hit the market and made a fortune in commissions."

"What does that mean?"

Joe shrugged. "Maybe something, maybe nothing. Could be the market is hot."

Anastasia frowned, reading Joe's screen. "Forward that list to me, will you?"

The line inched forward until they stood in front of the pastry case. "Sure is busy in here," Declan said to Sophia. "Scones must be flying off the shelves."

Instead of the expected smile, Sophia barely made eye contact. Dark circles framed her eyes, and sweat beaded across her upper lip. "'Morning. What can I get you?"

Joe ordered a macchiato, then offered to treat the others. Anastasia asked for drip coffee and a cinnamon bun. Declan eyed the case before ordering a cherry Danish to go with his latte. The trio paused their investigative talk until, drinks in hand, they were back on the sidewalk.

"Did Sophia seem...different?"

Anastasia sipped from her cup. She winced. "Too hot," she said. "I don't know. Maybe a bit...overwhelmed?"

"I've got to jet," Joe said, eyes still on his small screen. He downed half his drink. "If I'm gone too long, people notice."

Declan nodded. "I get that. You have a presence."

Joe started a slow jog, pointing back at Declan. "Taking that as a compliment," he said, before turning at the next corner.

"How's the new job?"

"Loving it," Anastasia said. "And hey, how about I bring a

drone over one of these days? I know you want to see one in action."

"Very cool. I could use some cheering up after today."

They'd reached the Ram & Rose. Sturrock was inside, bent over a board stretched between two sawhorses. From the window, they watched him saw through the wood. A chunk fell to the ground.

"How's the project coming?"

"Been at it three days," Declan said. "Going to bleed me dry, but it's looking good."

"I bet he could rebuild your stairs," Anastasia said.

Declan grimaced. "He could, but I need him to finish here first. I've got to get the shop in order so I can sell more plants so I can pay him for the privilege of selling said plants. Not sure how to afford more projects, let alone feed Lyncus."

"Don't worry," Anastasia said. She clapped Declan on the back. "If you go bankrupt, we'll have an all-out war over who gets your cat."

A couple hundred dollars lighter, Declan trudged home, Lyncus in his pack.

At the driveway to 1214, he paused.

Heated discussion came from the front of the house. Declan snuck around the side of the house until he was near the porch. Pressing himself flat against the siding, he listened.

"And I'm telling you," a woman's voice said, "you're not to be on the property."

"I'm just looking," said a man. "That's not illegal, is it?"

"This is private property—"

"Of a dead woman," the man said. The woman gasped, and the man backpedaled. "Look, I don't mean any disrespect, and I won't touch anything. I just wanted to take a peek, that's all. Might want to buy the place."

"People still live here," the woman said. "I'm calling the cops."

At this, Declan stepped around the corner. The woman from the Historical Society held a phone to her head. To her left, a younger man in a *Storia Brewing* T-shirt shook his head as she spoke to an operator. The man had a pair of sunglasses hanging from his neck, the ends connected by a red strap. He wore a pair of black rain boots and a waxed horseshoe mustache.

The man was the first one to see Declan. "Who are you?"

"I live here," Declan said, forgetting to hide that fact. From inside the pack, Lyncus chirruped in an echoed confirmation.

The woman—*Thatcher, was it?* Declan tried to remember —hung up the phone. "An officer is on the way, so you'd best get going."

"Oh, really?" The man tapped at his own phone, then met Thatcher's eyes. "I'm shaking with fear."

The woman glared, then gestured to Declan. "See? I told you someone still lived here."

The man sneered. "I did my homework. He's not the owner. She's gone."

A patrol car rolled up on the curb. The three people on the lawn watched as Rooney stepped out of the car. Declan closed his eyes and cursed the fates under his breath.

Rooney strutted forward like a fox in a hen house. "What have we got here?"

"This man," the woman said, pointing at Mr. Mustache, "was peeking into Jessica's house. I saw him. Sneaking around like he's casing the place."

"Now, Mrs. Thatcher, there could be a perfectly reasonable explanation for Mr. Wainwright's presence."

"You *know* him?"

"Hamilton Wainwright," the man said, extending a hand. Thatcher only pursed her lips.

Rooney said, a chuckle at the edge of his voice. "He's a brewer. *Storia* hosts the policeman's ball each year. Of course I know him."

"Well..." the woman stumbled over her words. "Tell *Mr. Wainwright* he can't be here. I don't see a *For Sale* sign anywhere. Jess wouldn't want random people," she spit out the word like a sour grape, "trampling her yard."

"Now, now," Rooney said. "We all know how much Jessica loved this place. If she were here, she would want the house to find a new owner who loved it as much as she did."

"If she were..." Declan muttered the words, confused by the officer's logic.

"And I would love it," Hamilton added.

"Even mentioned she'd consider selling," Rooney continued, "if it meant she'd finally get that restaurant of hers."

"Yeah," Hamilton said, "I remember the same."

"Lying's a sin," Thatcher said. "You never talked to Jessica Black one day of your life."

"Maybe not," Hamilton said. "But she sure loved visiting the brewhouse, didn't she? Bit too much, some think." He stared pointedly at the back yard, shaking his head.

"Come on, now, Mr. Wainwright," Rooney said, interrupting the burst of rage at Thatcher's lips. He put his hand on Hamilton's shoulder and escorted him toward the sidewalk. "You've had a peek. Get your finances sorted, get an agent. I'm sure there'll be a line out the door wanting this beauty, and you'll want to be in it."

"I'll be a decent landlord," Hamilton said over his shoulder to Declan. "You'll see."

"Like hell he will," Thatcher said. She planted herself on the lawn in a wide stance.

At his patrol car, Rooney paused. "Now Bernie, we all cherished Jess, but she's gone. Unless the historical society can afford the place, and I hope you all can, it's a beautiful place, you need to get used to the idea of a new owner. It's only a matter of time." He turned to Declan and lowered his sunglasses. He pointed to the remains of the stairs. "I don't know what happened here, but you'd better clean this up. If you trash the place, you could be held liable." He replaced the black lenses over his eyes and flashed them both a wide grin. "You two have a great day," he said, and ducked into his car.

"What a prick," the Thatcher woman said, glaring.

Declan stepped to her side. "Which one?"

"Exactly. Now come with me. I've got something to show you."

SEVENTEEN

Declan followed Thatcher around the building, away from the wide stone steps that led to the front entryway. At the back stood a single door. Next to it was a trash bin tagged in yellow spray paint.

"*Try harder?*"

Thatcher rolled her eyes. "Would have appreciated some devilish sign or a proper insult. Something to get torn up over. But do-gooding? It's like they ran out of angst before the paint was up."

The woman opened the door and braced it against one shoulder. "I'm Bernadette—Bernie—by the way."

"Declan," he said, nodding in greeting as he entered the building.

"We're officially closed up for the night, but I wanted to show you a tick of history." The door slammed closed behind him with weighted finality. "New clothes?"

Declan looked down at his navy sweater and gray slacks. "These are more my style. My family means well, but...they aren't the best at picking gifts."

"Another way loved ones try to force their influence. Say it's for you, but really it's pleasing themselves."

Declan didn't comment, afraid she'd ask more about his family. He continued to follow Bernie as she led him up a back set of stairs to a short hallway, past two tiny offices, one covered in paperwork, the other spartan and clean, and into the lobby of the building. "This place is huge," he said in reverence.

"Used to be City Hall," Bernie said. "Built in nineteen oh-four. Would have loved to live here back then. Those were the days when Astoria was a wild place with more drama than a bag of cats." The woman wound her way through the exhibits without flipping on a light switch. Declan stayed close, eyeing the lifelike displays. "Promise you'll come back when you've an afternoon to devote to your education," she directed.

"I will," Declan said, stopping in front of a display of items from a fur trapper's encampment. There was so much nuance in the human timeline, so many ways lives changed with each generation.

"Folks from here come by for our special exhibits, and tourists love it all. We added some special spots for kids, too." They'd taken a second flight of stairs, the wide, polished wood gleaming in the dim lighting. "Ah," Bernie said. "Here we are."

Bernie flicked on a tiny flashlight attached to her keychain. She aimed the beam at a wall of photographs, drawing the line of light across the vintage imagery. Halfway down the line, she stopped, stepping to the side so Declan could get a better look.

Declan recognized the location of the photograph in an instant—Jessica's house. There were different pots on the front steps and no garage, but the house was the same. From the steps leading up to the porch to the widow walk, the home held its identity with pride. On the short slope of the lawn, a woman stood with a little girl leaning into her side. The woman wore a long skirt and a blouse with a high collar and sleeves puffed at the shoulder. Her hair was twisted up and pinned at the top of her head. Despite the exhaustion on her features, the woman had kind eyes that held steady on the cameraman. The girl peered out from behind her mother's skirt with youthful shyness. The placard underneath the photograph read, "A cannery worker and her daughter. Image by H. P. Black."

Declan stared at the photograph, again in awe of the still frame in time. He pointed at the woman. "Is that...?"

Bernie nodded. "Lilly and Zelda Black. Jess's great-grandmother and grandmother. Lilly worked at the canneries while Hank was out at sea. Got something else. This way."

Back in the lobby, Bernie extracted a scrapbook from a shelf. She hefted it onto an acrylic bookstand before opening it to flip through the pages. While she searched, Declan let his attention stray to the building's architecture. Their every movement echoed in the grand chamber.

"Here we are," Bernie said. She'd opened to a selection of pages from a picnic on the front lawn. "This was from one of our Know Your Neighbor nights. Happened to be the fortieth anniversary of our occupation of this-here spot, so we funded ice cream on the grass for kids. One of our interns interviewed folks with family history in the town, and Jess was one of them." She turned the page to reveal an image cut from the newspaper. Bernie tapped at the picture. In the frame, the sun shone behind Jess as she stood in front of her house with a giant wedge of watermelon in one hand, a picture of a woman with delicate features and gray hair in the other. Below the image was a caption:

Jessica Black, fourth generation Astorian, holds a photo-graph of Zelda Black, her fraternal grandmother.

"Fraternal?"

Bernie nodded. "Zelda bucked conventions at every turn. Refused to name the father when she turned up pregnant one day. When Hank died, it was just the two women, one half grown, and that little boy in the end. Didn't matter to Lilly, though. She loved Zelda's son like names didn't matter. When he died, Zelda took in Jess's momma despite the two of them fighting like cats and dogs. The drink carried Molly off, poor thing."

Declan stared at the photo of Jess, smiling as though without a care in the world.

"Got a bit of her story in the article," Bernie said, tapping the page.

Declan skimmed the text.

From a long line of cannery workers and fishermen, Jessica's father died in a tragic accident when the *Orchard II* capsized off the coast. She is the remaining member of one of Astoria's founding families and plans to continue the legacy.

"This house holds my memories, my family," Ms. Black said. "It's how I stay connected to them, no matter what happens. Astoria is full of treasured homes, and we owe it to history to keep those stories alive."

When Declan looked up, Bernie met his gaze. "That place meant something to that poor girl. She wouldn't have sold it to save her life."

"I've got nothing." Maeve lit a stick of incense and set it on the windowsill of the studio. The thin stream of smoke snaked upward.

"Me either," Joe said. He'd folded forward, stretching his hands to grab the back of his massive feet. "Dry as a bone."

"We have to do something," Declan said. "That brewer was all but drooling on the place this morning."

"Brewer?" Anastasia slid on a pair of socks and sat cross-legged on a cushion. They were waiting for Cate to start the official meeting.

"Hamilton," Declan said. "From Storia Brewing. Was in the yard casing the place. Rooney made him leave but he walked the yard like he'd been there before."

"Maybe Hamilton rigged your stairs," Joe said, sitting upright.

"Rigged them to do what?" Cate entered, her hair dripping wet from the outdoors. She set down a bag filled with steaming white containers. "Bow Thai was out of Tom Kha, but they had a mango special and threw in some extra salad rolls."

"Fall off the garage and nearly get me killed," Declan answered. He watched the others fish through the boxes to make selections before choosing one of his own. His mouth watered at the scent of the Thai food as he reached for a set of chopsticks. Declan slotted the wooden sticks between his fingers, mirroring Joe. But where their giant of a friend snapped up chunks of vegetables with ease, his sausage-sized fingers deft and nimble, Declan sprayed Maeve with rice and dropped a salad roll into the soup.

Anastasia swallowed her mouthful of Pra Ram. "I'm ninety-nine percent certain that it was no accident. I scoped out the boards. What I don't get is why anyone would want to hurt Declan."

"I do," Maeve said. They all looked at her and she flushed. "What? If you want to catch a creep, think like a creep. Phoebe said no one can evict Declan until the end of his lease. No Declan, no lease."

"Brilliant and resourceful. I need to meet your Phoebe," Declan said.

Anastasia beamed. "I certainly agree with that."

"Then why not go after him at work?" Joe pondered this question, tapping his chopsticks on the side of his container. "He's there by himself most of the time."

"Hey," Declan said, giving the man a playful shove. Joe didn't budge. "I'm *trying* to get more customers. Sturrock's almost done with the kitchen. Now that I'm fairly certain I won't electrocute myself or anyone else in daily operations, I can start marketing. Business license for donuts came through, but I've got to pass the health inspection."

"Oooh," Cate said. "Let's throw a party—a Grand Opening! I love parties. I'll invite everyone I know." She dug into her box and extracted a shrimp. "Are you thinking sleek and sophisticated or more shabby chic?"

"Am I...I guess I hadn't got that far."

"Couldn't hurt," Maeve said. She poured deep red liquid into Declan's water bottle. "And it might help. Make a night of it. Maybe team up with a local winery." She rotated the bottle in her hands. "Like Buoy Vines."

"Cute label," Anastasia said, holding out her water bottle.

Cate nodded in rapid agreement with Maeve. "There could be games, prizes. And those special sticks they put in drinks with little seashell toppers?"

"Swizzle," Joe said. "Invented on a plantation in the West Indies in the eighteenth century." Joe shrugged at Anastasia's raised eyebrow. "What? I like rum."

"Yes, those!" Cate shifted from foot to foot in her excitement. She stepped to the front window of Mudra to take a peek at Ram & Rose. "Come on, Declan. Let's put it together. Pleeeease?"

"I'll think about it," Declan said, and he would. The idea of a shop full of people, all eyes on him, was unnerving, but so was the need to return home well ahead of schedule because he'd failed at his great experiment. "I will, I promise."

Maeve set the now empty bottle near the door. "Let's get things started, shall we?" She pulled out the whiteboard and leaned it against the mirrors. They had one suspect in the Loathing quadrant and that name was crossed out.

"I got this," Joe said. He scrambled to his feet and strode over to the board. In red capital letters, he added HAMILTON to the Loot quadrant. "Who else?"

"Just saying, it could still be random..." Maeve trailed off to dig into her own box.

Joe wrote RANDOM in the middle of the board. "Probably not love or loathing, but you never know."

"We're missing two categories, at least." Cate cracked her fortune cookie and extracted a message. "You will win the hearts of friends and neighbors. Huh, good enough." She tossed the cookie pieces into her mouth.

"She had that date with Steve," Declan said.

"She what?" Joe's marker hand hovered over the board. "I didn't know this."

Declan cast his eyes to the floor. "She'd marked it on her calendar at work. Then when I had to go in the house to fix the breaker situation, I found the same details written on the back of his business card."

"That slimy leech!" Anastasia stabbed her fork in the air. "Takes a girl out to get to her house. I see how this goes."

"Hold up," Declan said as his head spun. "That's a quick leap."

"Think about it," Anastasia said, pointing the fork at Declan. "He flirts with her and asks her out. Tries to figure out if she's willing to sell. Finds out she isn't. Turns up the charm to see if he can *convince* her through other means."

"More wine and dine?"

"By killing her," Cate said, considering the situation.

"We know Steve wasn't doing too hot until lately," Joe said. "Maybe he'd shifted his strategy."

"We need more information on Steve," Cate said. "Have you got anything?"

Joe shook his head. "We reported his death, that's about it. I'll write it down," Joe said, adding Steve to the Lust box. "And check in with Harvey to see if there has been any other news. I have heard that more and more people love the column, though."

"Uh, thanks," Declan said.

Cate selected another shrimp. "I heard two checkout clerks talking about it at the store, and a man at the bank. Even down at the docks, they aren't using that page to wrap the fish and chips."

"We do have a handful of new submissions." Maeve waved the cards in the air.

A rapping sounded through the front door. Declan got up to answer. "Great timing. Here's our special guest."

Declan opened the door to reveal Paxton, a paper sack in hand. Pax thrust the sack at Declan. "Nanaimo bars," he said. "Mom says thanks for keeping me off the streets tonight and will you please remind me to text her when I'm on my way home so she knows when to expect me?" The teen rolled his eyes and unzipped his jacket.

"I'll take those." Joe snatched the bag from Declan. "These are some of my favorites!"

"Your friend brought snacks," Cate said. She winked at Pax, who blushed. "What a cutie."

Maeve added another cushion to the circle. "Have a seat. There's some food left, if you're hungry."

Pax approached and consulted the stuffed, round circle. He attempted to sit on the cushion but slid backward. He tried again, keeping his knees up. "Tim had clients over. From Japan—*in-ves-tors*. Mom made a huge dinner for them which took forever. I was so bored I ate until I was about to burst. All that talk of *land use, rehabilitation*, and *zoning* stole my appetite for dessert. When I left, they were drinking fancy sake in the living room."

Maeve frowned. "Pax, your stepdad wouldn't happen to be in real estate, would he?"

"Think so." Pax hunched forward, hugging his knees. "I don't know what all he does. I know he's been raking in money making deals all over the place. His phone rings non-stop and Mom says we're going to Fiji for Christmas."

Joe lifted both brows and nudged Declan toward the whiteboard. Declan frowned and gave a slight jerk of his chin.

"Just curious," Maeve said, giving Declan a look behind the teen's back. "Haven't seen ol' Tim Ashford in a while."

"These are great," Joe said, holding up a layered bar. "Give my appreciation to your mom."

Declan cleared his throat, then spoke. "I asked Mr. Knight to join us this evening," Declan said, drawing out his explanation with a pregnant pause, "due to the author of one of our questions."

"Oh?" Camille rearranged her limbs into a full lotus. She pulled her long hair in front of her shoulder and started to braid. "Do tell."

Maeve handed Declan the card. He cleared his throat and read the loopy handwriting. "Dear Advice Person—"

Joe wrinkled his nose. "Don't like that."

"Shhh," Maeve said.

Declan continued to read. "I'm a freshman. There's a guy I like, but I have no idea how to find out if he likes me. He's always hanging out with his friends and I'm too nervous to talk to him in front of all of them. What should I do?"

"Give him food," Joe said, licking his fingertips.

Anastasia tapped her forefinger against her chin. "Maybe

write him a note? You know, fold it in one of those fancy origami shapes like we used to."

"This is why I invited Pax," Declan said, passing the boy the card. "I want to know what he thinks."

Pax reread the question, moving his lips as his eyes scanned the words. He pressed his lips together, thinking, then shrugged. "She's going to have to suck it up and get it over with."

Cate echoed his words. "...suck it up?"

Anastasia chimed in. "Get over herself. Am I right?"

Pax nodded. "Pretty much. Thing is, if she can't talk to him with other people around, it won't work. His friends are a part of him. They're going to be around if anything happens. And those other ways are...too much."

A soft smile played on Declan's lips. "So, what should I tell this writer?"

Pax said, "Guys admire bravery. Any guy who's worth liking would think it's pretty great someone came to talk to him. Doesn't have to be anything big, just a 'Hey, how's it going?' Or 'Did you get the notes for Spanish?' Anything to get the ball rolling. If he talks, great. If not, then there's no physical proof of her crush and she can move on without embarrassment."

"I like it, the kid's smart," Joe said. "Might have to replace you."

"Funny," Declan said. "You haven't even paid me for my first gig, and I'm already ousted."

"Maybe he could do a young reader version," Anastasia said. "Couldn't hurt to have options."

Maeve tilted her chin. "Could be good. Get Joe new readers."

"I want to read the next one," Cate whined, reaching out to snatch a card from Maeve's hands.

Pax raised both eyebrows as his attention volleyed between

those in front of him. "Is this what you all do every Friday night?"

The adults stopped their chatter. Declan looked at his friends, the Bleeding Hearts, and smiled at Pax. "Yeah, pretty much."

"Kinda weird," Pax said. "But I like it."

Eighteen

"Special delivery," Cate called. She entered the plant shop with a bag in each hand. "Are you a halibut fan?"

"Depends. What's that?" Declan had finished unpacking his latest plant delivery onto the new shelving. He'd repurposed a few glass bowls from the bar's days to create height in the displays. This allowed him to make better use of space. He bumped one orchid against another, and a bloom fell off. "Son of a siren."

"What was that?"

Declan picked up the fallen blossom and twirled it between his fingers. "Oh, just something Pax says, to keep from swearing. Kind of rolls off the tongue."

"Yeah, if you don't know any si—" Cate began, then changed the subject. "Halibut is a fish. You know..." she pressed both palms together and waved them outward from her middle. "Might be the last catch of the season so I saved you some. Got a fridge?" She eyed the plastic sack, heavy with filets. "And a freezer?"

"In the kitchen," Declan said. He whipped out his phone

to add "how to cook halibut" to his research list, then hunted in a drawer for some wire.

Several minutes later, Cate emerged. Her damp hair was tied back in a customary braid. "Went out with the fellas to see what's biting," she said. "Got some dirt on Steve in addition to the fish."

"Tell me more," Declan said. He held out the fallen orchid blossom to her, two fine wires sticking out from his wrap job. "For your hair."

Cate took the gift. "I love it," she said, and wove the wires through her thick plait. Reminds me of when I visit Hawaii. Get all kinds of things stuck in my hair, but I've never minded the orchids. Too many tourists toss their leis into the ocean to make a wish. Such a silly waste," she said, looking at the blossom.

"You were saying?"

"Oh, yes. Steve has a boat at the docks. No one's been near it since he died. The guys were saying no one would want it now that it's haunted. No one local, anyway" Cate tucked the flower behind one ear and reached into the paper sack she'd left on the bar. She removed a stack of napkins, half of which she piled in front of Declan before creating her own stack. Her hands disappeared into the bag again.

"Haunted?" Grown fishermen scared of a personal water-craft was ludicrous in Declan's mind.

Cate withdrew two newspaper-wrapped bundles and set one on Declan's napkins before placing the other in front of herself. Declan stepped behind the bar and filled a couple of water glasses while she continued to talk. "Al said he heard bumps and clattering from it a couple nights this week. Random lights on. According to him, Steve's last sail was a disaster, then with the way he died...no one wants to take on that kind of luck. Fishermen are a superstitious bunch."

"I thought he drowned?" Declan pressed. He set the two

glasses in front of each of them, added a pair of forks and some salt and pepper shakers. Whatever Cate brought had a delicious aroma.

His surprise lunch date unwrapped her parcel. "Open yours," she said. "You'll love it."

Declan lifted the layers of newspaper to reveal several hunks of fried meat atop a bed of fries. Cate handed him a packet of malt vinegar and a couple that contained ketchup. "Dig in," she said, and took a bite. Declan followed suit.

"This is incredible," he groaned.

"One of my favorites," Cate said. "I'm a...sushi kind of girl. I like most of it raw, but halibut's the exception."

As the long-haired beauty chowed down, Declan observed her. The woman's sun kissed cheeks were smattered with freckles, the pupils of her green eyes circled in yellow. Her arms were lean and muscular. She was curvy and nimble, an athlete. Also of note, she showed no signs of attraction to Declan. Sure she was married, but that hadn't stopped thousands before her from throwing themselves at his feet. He wondered if these were platonic relationships—what he had with the Bleeding Hearts. Not every interaction had an undercurrent of romance.

"Anyway," Cate said, daubing more vinegar on her halibut. "They told me Steve was a championship swimmer in college. Used to swim every morning, even in the pissing down rain. Said it was good for him. I'm surprised I never saw him out there. The idea that an experienced seaman who could swim like a fish would drown is baffling at best, a curse at the worst."

Declan dipped a fry in ketchup. "Are the fishermen forming their own investigation club?"

Cate shook her head. "Coroner already ruled it a drowning and said that he'd been bobbing about for a while. They're lucky the sea lions didn't play catch with him."

From his position on the widow's walk, Declan watched Pax head up and over the hill. He'd claimed his house to be just over the ridge. The boy sent his mother the promised text, then saluted Declan as he trudged over the hill.

"I like that kid," Declan said.

"I do, too," Anastasia said. She huddled over a case of equipment, snapping parts together.

After saying goodnight to Pax, they'd ducked into Jess's house through the back door. Declan ignored the guilt of having pocketed the house key along with the key to the garage during the power outage. If anything else happened and he needed access, he would have it. The new owner would change the locks when they took over, he thought, so no harm in having access for a while.

Anastasia had balked at the ladder to the uppermost story but acquiesced when Declan volunteered to carry the case up for her.

"Beautiful spot," she said. "I can see why Jess liked it."

Declan didn't reply. Being on the narrow walkway, a chunk of railing still missing, was unsettling. He tried not to picture Jess's body splayed out in the grass. He faced the Columbia, its surface an eerie darkness. Lyncus waited near the edge of the walkway, licking one paw and rubbing it across his forehead as though several stories up was an everyday situation.

"Hey, meant to ask you," Anastasia started. "Would it be cool if my ex drops off our dog at your place? Just until I get off work. He's got to head to Portland for a meeting."

"Your...ex...dog...what?"

"We share custody of a dog. Uncle is his name. I know, that's a thing people on TV do," Anastasia said. "We just both love the little guy so much."

"I'm still back at ex."

Anastasia laughed. "Brody. We were married for a dozen years, about eight of them happy. Friends-ish, now. Anyway, when we weren't sure if we wanted kids, we adopted a dog from Maeve. Now we trade off every week—like a kid. Kinda nice for vacation purposes..." She trailed off. "Look it was a dumb idea, sorry for asking. It's just that I can't have a dog at work. But if Brody could leave him with you before he leaves, then I could come get him on my lunch and run him home. Normally the timing's better."

"Not a problem. Don't know much about dogs, but I've managed to keep the cat alive this long. How much harder can another animal be?"

"You're a life saver," Anastasia said. "Brody will bring him as soon as he docks."

"Docks?"

"He's a guide. Takes the wealthy out on whatever kind of adventure they want...within reason. Usually that's fishing. Brody's great for keeping gulls away from the amateurs who dangle their first catch like it's bait." Anastasia flicked a few switches, loaded up an app on her phone, and the drone, a machine the size of a serving platter, lifted from its rooftop launchpad. "And we're off!"

"It's quieter than I thought," Declan said. He kept his eyes on the whirring machine, its blinking white light a beacon.

Anastasia ran the device through a pattern of maneuvers in the yard. The device bobbed and whirred, landed, did a flip, then took off again. She handed her phone to Declan. "Here's the camera view. You can be the eyes of our operation."

Declan held the small screen displaying a patch of grass below. "Are we allowed to do this?"

"Fly a drone?"

"At night. To potentially spy on people," Declan said. The

screen followed the fence line as Anastasia skimmed it with the drone.

"Yes and no. I don't need a permit to fly for you over your own residence, but then things start to get tricky. I've got a license, and our drone is up to code, but we've still got to be careful. I won't be flying into anyone else's yard, just sticking to the streets and public areas. That I'm allowed to do."

"Reasonable," Declan said, ease settling in.

"I'm also using one of my personal drones, which is far more generic than those we have at work. If anything happens to it, there's no ties to me."

Declan's eyes were wide. "So, you think we'll see something good? This is far more exciting than I thought."

Anastasia laughed. "Covering my bases. Don't want to get fired from a job I just landed." Her eyes on the drone, Anastasia flew it out and over the street. She stuck the tip of her tongue out between her lips while she focused. "That said, you never know what will come into view."

"Any idea where we should look?"

"Flying kind of blind as far as that's concerned. I'll fly a pattern so it's easy to track."

Anastasia flew a zigzag, east to west. They spotted a couple making out in a car, someone smoking behind a dumpster, and a group of kids throwing French fries for the gulls. "Pretty mild night," she said.

Declan squinted, attempting to spot the drone in the sky. Through the camera, he watched bushes and trees rush by, a rainbow of parked cars below. "I see it," he said, triangulating. "It's by the Astor Building."

Anastasia nodded. "Coming up the backside of the brewery block now."

Declan watched through the screen as sidewalk squares fell away. Movement in the corner caught his eye. "Wait, back there," he said, aware of how misdirected that statement would sound. "I mean, by the corner of the building. I saw someone."

Anastasia brought the drone in a wide circle until a lone figure came into view. She peered at the phone in Declan's hands. "That's Hamilton Wainwright."

"Mr. Mustache, himself. Can you follow him?"

"I'll keep him in our sights but stay back a bit."

From the screen, Declan watched Hamilton zip up a black hoodie and lift the hood over his head. He shoved his hands in his pockets and walked at an easy pace, as though he had nowhere to be. At Exchange and 14th, he turned up the hill. Several houses down, he ducked into a yard. "Between the fences—there." Declan pointed to the screen.

Anastasia shook her head. "Can't go closer. Private property. I'll hang back."

Hamilton emerged moments later, stuffing his phone into his back pocket. He continued up the street a half block before ducking into another yard. He repeated this pattern for several more blocks.

"What is he doing?" Anastasia asked. "Can you tell?"

"Involves his phone, whatever it is," Declan said. "Taking pictures?"

At a street corner, he whirled. On camera, he stared straight at Declan and held up both middle fingers. "I think we've been spotted," Declan said.

Anastasia checked the screen. "Oh boy. All right, I'll bring her in."

Minutes later, the drone landed on the widow's walk in a gentle descent.

"Think he followed it?"

Anastasia shook her head. She collected the machine and began to disassemble the parts for storage. "Nope, I took too many turns at a decent speed."

"He was up to something," Declan said. "The question is what."

"Joe might be right," Anastasia said. "One Hamilton Wainwright is worth a second look."

A series of short yaps announced the Scottish terrier to the shop. The dog was followed in by a cheerful man holding the end of the leash. "Hi," the man said, holding out his hand. "I'm Brody. 'Stasia said you'd be expecting me?"

Declan's watering can was filled to the brim. He gave the man's hand a firm shake, willing the water not to slop over the sides. "Come on in. It's good to meet you."

"Great place you've got here. 'Stasia will be the first to tell you I don't get out much, so I could probably use a few plant buddies in the office. How long have you been open?"

"Not long," Declan said. He thought of playing tag in the grottos as a child. Stately rows of Italian Cypress lining the great halls. Tumbling over a bed of rose petals with— "Wait, what was that again?"

"I said I could use a few tips myself. Got any that would survive a bachelor who's gone for several nights in a row?"

Brody wasn't tall, but he was sturdy. He wore a flannel shirt with a pair of corduroy pants, the cuffs tucked into hiking boots. He was shabby, but clean, if a little scruffy about the chin.

"I'm thinking of a snake plant. Also known as a mother-in-law's tongue." Declan lifted a pot with large, flat leaves edged in yellow, the spires twisting upward. "Can definitely handle a little neglect, and they look great year-round."

"I'll take it," Brody said. He took out his wallet. "And thanks again for watching our dog."

"So, this is the little guy, then?" Declan regarded the pup. "Doesn't seem too tough." He thought of Maeve's wild pack.

"Aww, our Uncle's a very good boy—except around pigeons. Hates 'em."

Declan accepted the leash. The scruffy black dog snuffed at his shoes before turning a tight circle to settle on the ground, chin on his front paws.

"Just walked him, so he should be good for a bit. A little water, if you've got a dish, but he shouldn't need much else." Brody squatted to pat the dog. "See you next weekend, bud."

"I've never had a dog, but Anastasia said she wouldn't be long. I'm sure he'll be no trouble at all."

When Anastasia asked if Declan would watch Uncle until she got off work, he'd jumped at the chance. His great-uncle had made dog ownership look easy. Feed them decent food, give them a task, and show affection. Trying on the hat of a dog owner had appeal.

Declan was more worried about Lyncus, however. He was unsure how the cat would handle a temporary canine buddy. Instead of protesting, the cat lounged on the bar top where he could maintain watch over the new furry intruder.

Brody walked toward the door, his plant tucked under one arm. At the exit, he turned back. "Say, Stasia said your little group was discussing Steve Corey—the real estate agent? She and I loved watching those true crime shows once upon a time, so it makes total sense she'd be into detective work."

"Uh...yeah?"

"That man practically begged me to sell him the house when Stasia and I first decided to split. Said he had a big client looking for investment properties. Offered cash. I put him off. Never told 'Stasia about it. Feelings ran a bit too high back then. You know how that goes."

"Do I ever."

Nineteen

"I'm here with a delivery," Declan said, a massive autumnal flower arrangement in his hands. There were sunflowers and mums, eucalyptus sprigs, and a branch of magnolia leaves he'd clipped on his walk.

Pax had been more than willing to earn a little money by running an errand. Declan had needed to hurry, making do with fluffing up the bouquets Pax snagged from the grocery store. Waiting for Anastasia to collect Uncle gave Declan the time to assemble the arrangements. The dog yipped when Declan presented the final results of his artistry.

When Anastasia arrived, she was in full support of Declan's plan. She dropped him off at his first afternoon stop and wished him luck.

Now, Declan leaned over a Formica countertop, engaging with a woman wearing giant glasses and her hair in a tight knot atop her head.

"What is the delivery?"

Declan looked down at the bouquet, then to the woman. "They're flowers," he said. "In memoriam."

The woman blinked.

"Can I just give this to someone in management?"

With false talons decorated with rhinestones, the assistant tapped a few buttons on the office phone keypad before picking up the handset. "Mr. Jones? Delivery for you at the front desk." She sank the headset back into its cradle. "He'll be out shortly," she said. "You can have a seat."

Dismissed, Declan hefted the arrangement back into his arms and stepped away from the desk. Moments later, a man breezed into the lobby of Coastal Realty, a wide smile on his face. "Hello. And what have we here?" He held his hands out toward the bouquet, as though touching it were forbidden.

"This is for the agency. In recognition of the loss of a..." Declan consulted the card he'd made a half hour ago as though it wasn't his own handwriting on the order. "...Steve Corey. Oh, I'm so very sorry to hear that." He foisted the arrangement onto the man and stepped back.

"Oh, I see," said the man, his perma-smile slipping a bit. He looked around the lobby before setting the flowers on the glass coffee table. "Who...uh...sent them?"

"I believe it was one of your clients. A...um...uh. I'm sorry," Declan said, frowning at the tag. "I can't seem to read the name. When I get back to the shop, I'll find the invoice and call you. Will that be all right, Mr....?"

"Jones," said the man, offering Declan his card. "Steve was one of our agents."

"I see," Declan said, pocketing the card he had every intention of losing. He affected his best approximation of sad, turning down the corners of his mouth and blinking. "Was he here long?"

"Old Steve was a long-timer. At least, it sure seems like forever." Jones gave a slight shrug. "Probably would have retired from this place in another ten years. Was saving up for a new boat—said he'd call her Betty. Had it all picked out and everything. Poor guy."

"That's terrible. Did he leave a family behind?"

"An ex. Kids are grown, but it's still hard, you know?"

Declan didn't, but he nodded.

Jones slid his hands in his pockets and shrugged outward with his elbows. "Drowning. A real shame, and no small surprise."

"I'm sure everyone's at a loss. You all must be scrambling to keep up."

"Not really," Jones said. "Business as usual here at Coastal. Steve was in special projects. Only had one client. Guessing this"—he gestured at the flowers—"is from them. Anyway, thanks for the delivery." Jones turned back to the doorway, whistling, and was gone.

AC/DC blared from the garage-style doors. Inside, giant steel tanks held court, tubing and hoses everywhere in between. A dozen customers occupied picnic tables in a large courtyard, soaking up what little sun poked through the afternoon clouds. Declan brought his dish of succulents to the bar.

"What can I get you and your, uh...little plant friends?" The man at the taps had shaggy brown hair, a hibiscus tattooed on his neck, and the easy smile of someone unconcerned by anything other than the present moment.

"Thanks, but I'm actually here to deliver this. Would Hamilton be around?"

"Sure, I'll get him. Who should I say is here?"

Declan smiled. "His future tenant."

The weasely man with the two-pronged mustache surfaced from somewhere behind the massive tanks. Declan held out his offering. "Thought I'd bring this to say no hard feelings about the other day."

"Uh...thanks?" Hamilton stared down at the selection of

succulents as though they were bacteria growing in a Petri dish.

"I wondered if you might display it here. At the brewery. I've got a couple cards to go with it. I could come by once a week and take care of it. If you like it, I could bring you some other plants, too."

Hamilton read Declan's business card. "And what's in it for you...Declan?"

"Almost free advertising," Declan said.

The brewer tapped the card on the bar, thinking. "I like it. How about I throw in a pint a week?"

"Of beer?" Declan hadn't considered a barter.

Hamilton smiled, a smirk in his upper lip. "That's what we got. You hear that, Mick?"

"I got you," said Mick from behind the bar. "This man drinks for free. Should I tell the boss, or will you?"

"Oh," Declan said. "I'm sorry. Sounds like I should have been bugging someone else."

"Naw," Hamilton said, brushing off Declan's protest. "Reggie trusts my judgment. Letting me pick the spot for our expansion, isn't he?"

Mick held up both hands in submission and grabbed a rack of dirty pint glasses before disappearing toward the back.

"Thanks for this. Looks cool on the bar like that. And uh, hey," Hamilton began, leaning close to Declan. "Sorry about the other day. No disrespect meant to Jess. Things got a little out of hand."

Declan shook his head. "Don't worry about it. That's why I came over—to make peace." *So long as you don't cut down my new stairs, you slimy jerk.*

"Look, I feel bad about Jess. I really do. She was sweet."

Declan's attention perked up. "You knew her?"

Hamilton nodded. "Had me collecting spent grain for her to use in her bread. Said it saved her a fortune and made for a solid loaf. I tried the stuff, and it was really good. She was pinching every penny, trying to save up for that restaurant."

"Sounds like her," Declan said. "Had big dreams."

"I know she would have turned that closet of a kitchen into a restaurant if she could've. But Sophia wouldn't budge. Bet she's regretting that now. The price of everything is jumping higher, and I'm not sure who'll stay in business at this rate."

"I'm doing my best," Declan said. He took in the beer counter, the row of taps, and the machinery behind Hamilton. "Looks like y'all are doing great. You're planning to expand?"

"If the boss plays his cards right," Hamilton says. "Started distilling and finally have some decent products. Astoria could use a cocktail place, like a speakeasy, and we've got the goods to make it happen. I'm trying to hook the boss up with a great spot, but you know how it is. Not everyone knows how to visualize."

"So I've learned," Declan said, and fought back the smile that played on his lips. He pointed at a picture propped near the register. In it, Hamilton and three other men held up their catches for the camera. "You're a fisherman?"

"Yeah," Hamilton said. "On my days off—when I can get them."

"I hear that," Declan said. He patted the bar mat twice. "I'll see you next week."

"What did the fabulous Phoebe find?"

Declan clutched the phone between his ear and shoulder. With one hand, he selected a pothos vine and with the other made a clean snip. He cut the strand into individual leaves before tucking each stem into water-filled highball glasses.

Declan had found several unopened cases of glassware under the bar, most intact.

"Hamilton worked at Coastal. For all of three months. He was an intern, assembling a portfolio."

Declan set the glasses on a shelf. He switched on the grow light above. The blue and red lighting beamed down on the leaves. "What happened there?"

"Not one hundred percent certain, but one Hamilton Wainwright has a suspended realtor license. Got a DUI."

"Guessing potential clients don't want to be driven around by someone who's intoxicated." Declan switched his phone to the other ear. "A career that was over before it started."

"Uh...Declan. Any chance you can meet me at your place?"

"Why?"

"The city hired me to get footage for some promos and I'm out here at the park. I'm looking at an image of one former realtor standing in Jess's back yard. And he's got company."

The entire way home, Declan swore under his breath. He'd meant to put Hamilton at ease, not encourage him further.

Declan ran-walked the last few blocks, cutting across a lawn and ducking through a back alley. When the house came into view, so did the figures of Hamilton and two other men, all in the front yard. Declan dove behind a boxwood and crouched, listening.

"What do you mean a sale is in the works?" This was Hamilton, his voice high and whiny.

"I represent a client with significant interests in the area.

I'm not able to disclose the details. When one has resources, certain processes become...smoother."

"But it hasn't even hit the market. Her estate can't be settled."

"Fredrick, check over there," the man said.

"I see one," the other man said. There was a rattling as he dragged something across the yard.

"This isn't over," Hamilton said. "I'm making some calls."

"It's your time," the man said, coolly.

Declan froze as footsteps approached the other side of the fence from where he crouched.

"I don't know," Hamilton said. There was a pause. "Two suits. One's a lawyer...I told you, I have no idea. Okay...okay. Got it. Tonight."

Hamilton's voice drew closer with every response. Declan dashed through the side yard of the house, flattening himself against a wall. Hamilton passed, his focus on the conversation coming through the speaker of his phone.

The brewer growled into the microphone. "All I need is the name."

Declan crawled back to the boxwood, waited fifteen minutes, then took the long way around the block. He scurried up to the house only to spot a letter taped to the door to his apartment, a story and a half off the ground.

Twenty

"It's not an eviction notice," Maeve said, tutting over the official document. She flattened the damp paper over the bar and dabbed at it with a small towel. "It's a Notice to Comply."

"Close enough," Declan said. He shoved both hands in his hair and paced the shop. "What do I do?"

Lyncus sat in Maeve's lap, and she stroked him from head to tail. "Make repairs and all will be fine."

"I've got thirty days to make this nightmare go away. There's no telling who will own the place then."

"Come on," Maeve said. "Let's get some strong coffee and sugar in our veins. We'll get this figured out."

Five minutes later, they stood in front of a pair of shopfront windows.

It was official. Jess's kitchen was no longer. The left window still held the two-foot, golden letters of its former occupant, faded against the glass. Within the shop, mixing bowls stood empty on the countertop. Oils and spices filled a wire rack as though their use was imminent.

The right hand windows were covered in brown paper, a

white sign taped to the glass: *Another TurnKey property on its way!* The small brick building was empty, a pair of seagulls eyeing its visitors from the rooftop.

"Looks like I'm going to have to take a rain check on that scone," Declan said.

The breeze teased some of Maeve's hair loose from its clip as she stared at the windows. "Damn," she whispered. "Not a word from the old crone. Just...gone."

"But what, exactly, was that breaking point?"

Declan bumped into an open drawer and dropped his scissors. One blade nicked the leather of his shoe, narrowly missing his big toe. "Godsdamnit," he said, then checked to ensure he was alone. He slipped off the shoe to better assess the damage.

A graceful figure tipped into the shop through the open top half of the door. "Is this the location of the famous Ram & Rose? It's in my guidebook as a must visit."

Declan froze, loafer in hand. The voice grated his spine like ice. All the color drained from his face as he turned around.

"Mother," he said, and plastered on a wide grin. "What brings you here?" He stepped back into his shoe and hustled over to unlatch the door.

"Oh, come now. What mother needs an excuse to visit a beloved child? Thought I'd drop by and see what you've been up to these last few weeks."

Declan leaned out to ensure no witnesses were behind her before flipping the sign and locking the door.

"Isn't this place adorable? It's all so...dark and...rustic." She stood in the center, taking in the plants. "And a bar," she said, taking a seat on a stool. She tossed a burlap sack onto the bar top. "Such charm. Harmonia picked the perfect spot, didn't she?"

"Mother," Declan said, standing at her side. "You really should have let me know you were coming."

"And spoil all the fun? Tosh. I wanted to see your little place. Besides, I've never been to Astoria. Who doesn't enjoy a spontaneous jaunt to the coast?"

Declan stared at this iteration of his mother. In a blue satin suit that hugged this form, she perched on the stool, tan heels hooked over the footrest. Auburn ringlets tumbled to her shoulders and crimson lipstick accentuated her mouth. His mother had a knack for flashy appearances.

"I got your present," Declan said, hoisting Lyncus up from his nap in the deep windowsill. The cat meowed in protest. He plunked the animal on his mother's lap.

Lyncus stretched along her legs, arching his back and kneading into her thighs before settling in the dip of her skirt. His mother held her hands aloft, as though afraid to touch the creature. When he purred, she gave him a brief one-two pat on the head.

"Yes, well. Couldn't have you out here all alone. Do you like him?"

"You mean to say, do I like that you're spying on me through a cat?"

"What are you talking about?" She made a show of checking the cat from several angles.

Declan sighed, tired of the pantomime. "Why are you here?"

"Can't a mother be curious about her son's life? Besides, it's not like you've sent us any news." She pouted, the picture of a parent put out by an inconsiderate child.

"And just how was I supposed to do that—beam something into the sky?" Declan was frazzled, an unwelcome sensation.

"I'm here now, and I want to hear everything." She leaned

back, resting her elbows on the polished wood. "Including what you were doing just now."

Declan sighed. The last thing he wanted to do was detail his life through the latest frustrations. "I was working," he said, holding up the scissors. "If I don't keep the plants pruned, they get leggy. And that's in between helping customers."

His mother made a show of twisting her head to search the store. "Darling, I don't see anyone in here. Now take a seat and spill on your new life. Start with the dating scene." She waggled her perfect eyebrows.

Resisting his mother, of all mothers, was futile. Reluctant, Declan lumbered over to the other stool and took a seat. "Fine. I will give you a brief update, and then I need to get back to work." Declan summarized his arrival in the ridiculous suit and the death of Jess.

His mother's eyes went wide. "How *tragic*. Like an opera playing out in real time. How absolutely stimulating."

"You know how things work around here better than I do. People die every day."

His mother frowned, the crinkle above her right eye the only suggestion of her age. "The yoga people sound delightful, at least."

Declan considered the crew. "You know, they're the best part of this place. I wouldn't have made it without them."

"Maybe I could meet them?"

Declan shook his head. "No. Absolutely not. You cannot meet my friends. What would I say? They'll ask questions I can't answer. You'll get me in trouble."

Lyncus jumped down from his mother's lap as she stood to brush off her dress. "I am aghast you think so little of me— my own son. I only came to pledge my support."

Declan sneered. "Support? You don't want me here, admit

it. You want me to come crawling home, tail between my legs—"

"You've grown a tail?" She wrinkled her nose and peered at his backside.

"It's an expression," Declan said. "It means you want me to admit I've lost and you've won. That my business is limping along, that everything is terrible. Well, it's not true. I have friends. And while traffic has been light at the shop, it'll be here in full force around the holidays, I'm told. Meanwhile, I'll throw an Open House and see what happens."

"Ooh, a human party! Can I come?"

"No," Declan said. "Look, you wouldn't like it. We'll have cheap hors d'oeuvres and boxed wine. I'll have to engage in small talk about plants until I pass out."

She made a face. "You're right, I'd hate that."

"See, that's the thing. It's not about what you would like, it's the reality of this life. *My* life. There's no time for made-up drama. I'm probably going to get evicted, and I've got to try to find a new place that accepts a pet, thanks to you. That's something humans go through. People here can't just exist how they want, when they want."

"You're about to lose your home?" His mother's manicured brows lifted, two perfect arches across her face.

"I can handle it," Declan said, and threw his hands up into the air. "I will handle it. What I don't need is you stepping in."

"Mothers meddle. It's how we show our love."

Declan crossed his arms. "I'm learning love is in the reception, not the intent."

"You've also learned to question me, I see," she said dryly.

Declan exhaled a slow breath. "Please don't make this about you."

"So much for the joy of a surprise visit." She reached for the purse she'd carried in and replaced her oversized black sunglasses on her face. The gigantic circular lenses gave her the look of a housefly. "Apparently you don't need me anymore. You're perfectly happy to implode your existence and wallow in human suffering." She glanced around the shop and added, "And *work*."

"I *enjoy* working. It gives me satisfaction. I get up every day and go to the same places. Get coffee and Thai takeout. Wash my clothes so I can wear them again another day. I have problems and I try to fix them. I talk with my friends about their problems. Go to yoga. There's this whole thing we do with wine and love letters and mysteries. It's really nice." As Declan spoke, he warmed from within, as though stoking a hearth. "I need this, Mom. Please understand. It's not about going against you, it's about doing something for me."

In the doorway, his mother regarded him, a small pout on her face. "You know, motherhood is cruel, in its way. You're never free of worry, yet your children never appreciate what their freedom costs you." Then she disappeared through the door.

Declan picked up the brown sack she'd left and rushed to the doorway to check the sidewalks. She was gone. He opened the drawstring to find two pounds of raw coffee beans.

Outside the door to Mudra was an envelope tacked to the corkboard, Declan's name scrawled across the front. Next to this was a new card.

TWENTY-ONE

"This is the confession of a coward—"

"Wait!" Cate shouted from the entryway. "I've almost got my shoes off—don't start yet!"

"Should have been in class," Maeve called back.

Cate entered, a box in one hand. The cardboard was stamped with the shape of a shrimp. She opened the container to reveal a selection of sushi and winked at Declan. As the others oohed and aahed over the presentation, Cate passed out sets of bamboo chopsticks to everyone.

"I brought something to share, too." Joe followed in behind Cate. He extracted a few handfuls of fungi with frilly, pale-yellow tops from the kangaroo pouch on the front of his sweatshirt. "Don't eat those—yet. Take them home."

"Chanterelles!" Anastasia picked up a mushroom. "Absolute beauties. Where did you find them?"

Joe beamed at Anastasia. "I have my spots."

"I've always wanted to go mushroom hunting," Anastasia said. "Bundle up and head into the forest. Come back and cook something fabulous."

Joe's eyes shone. "I could take you sometime..."

"I'd love that," Anastasia said, and Joe beamed.

Declan consulted a mushroom. "They're very cool looking." Brushed with earth, the chanterelles smelled of dry leaves. "Will someone tell me what to do with them?"

Cate and Maeve exchanged a look. "They don't have mushrooms in Washington anymore?"

Declan blinked. "No. I mean, of course they do. Just not this...fresh."

Maeve grimaced and pushed a significant portion of the chanterelles toward Declan.

"Sauté them in a little butter," Anastasia said. "Bit of salt and pepper, some thyme. Got to try them as they are, first. Then go for omelets."

"Right," Declan said. He scooped the chanterelles into a pile and considered his latest blunder.

"All right, let's get down to business." Cate unsheathed her chopsticks from the paper wrapping. She snapped them apart and rubbed them against each other with frantic friction. After arranging the implements between her fingers, she snagged a piece of sushi—a slice of fish atop a small pile of rice—from a box with deft chopstick skills. Declan watched her daub the morsel into a green paste she'd squirted into the box. Cate popped the piece in her mouth.

"Time to read," Anastasia said.

Declan studied his own chopsticks. They clicked together in his hands, useless at picking up anything other than air. He set them aside and picked up the letter. The others dug into the feast while Declan again unfolded the sheaf of paper resting atop an envelope.

Joe asked, "When did you find it?"

Maeve said, "Before I opened."

Declan cleared his throat and read

"This is the confession of a coward, something that would bring my family shame, but none of them are left to know it.

When you find this, I'll be long gone, headed to Arizona and a new life. I picked out a little condo in a retirement village. Maybe those folks will like my scones. I loved this community, but things have changed. When Zelda found out about the cancer, she made me promise to watch over her granddaughter. Instead, I was jealous. When that man came around, I suggested Jessica might be interested in selling. I thought if she could afford a restaurant, we'd be out of each other's way. The night before she died, we argued, but she wouldn't listen to me. Before you head off to tell the police, I already did. I didn't kill her, but her ghost haunts me just the same. In the end, I sold my place instead. I wish you luck and have included my family's recipe for old-fashioned donuts."

Declan set the letter on the floor for all to see. "I didn't know Sophia knew Jess's grandmother."

Maeve sighed, then plucked a salmon roll from among the sushi. "They were the same age, and Astoria is much bigger now than it was decades ago."

"Why tell you?" Joe held both chopsticks in a fist. "No offense, but it's not like you were the best of friends."

Declan folded the letter and tucked it back in the envelope. "Guilt is a powerful motivator." He frowned at his name on the front. "A burden shared is a burden halved."

"Are we going to talk about the card now?" Maeve looked at Declan, who pressed his lips together. "It's not that I won't miss the Pastry House and Sophia, but that ship has sailed."

Cate fished around in a container for a slice of pickled ginger. "Go on, read it, Declan."

"'Bout time," said Joe. "Was worried we wouldn't fill the next column."

"There's no way this one's going in the paper," Declan said.

Anastasia extracted a chocolate bar from her purse. She snapped the wrapped bar in several places before placing it in the middle of their circle and peeling back the paper. She selected a chunk. "Out with it, Declan. Even if it's not very good."

"You can always spice it up for the paper," Cate said. "A little...poetic license."

Declan pulled the card from his back pocket and read.

Stop looking for what you aren't meant to find.

Cate blinked. "Is that it?"

"What's that supposed to mean?"

Maeve recrossed her legs. "Is it a fortune cookie or a threat?"

Anastasia frowned. "You think it's a threat?"

Declan shrugged and passed the note to Joe, who read it and passed it to Cate. "I don't know. I'm fairly sure someone isn't too happy with us."

Sushi consumed, the group packed up and headed out into the night. Anastasia ducked into her hatchback, Cate set off for the pier, and Joe lumbered off toward the wooded side of town.

Declan waited for Maeve as she locked up for their walk home together, a new routine.

"Have you ever been propositioned?" Declan asked.

Maeve dropped her keys into her purse and slung the bag over her shoulder. She lifted her brows at Declan. "Come again?"

"From someone wanting to buy this place," he said.

"For a moment, I thought we were about to have a very different conversation." Maeve set off down the sidewalk. Her quick footsteps set the pace. "I have," she said. "Every few months or so. I'm one of the few businesses that doesn't lease. You're one of the others." She arched a brow at him.

Declan hung his head, walking with hands in his pockets. He kicked at a stone. They passed a house with a group of pumpkins on the front porch, a wreath of colorful autumn leaves on its door. "I'm..." Declan searched for the word. "... disappointed."

"In?" Maeve trudged up the incline alongside him.

"Well, Sophia, for one." He lifted his head to look at Maeve. "And myself, for another."

"You've hardly sold out. And whatever this pact was that Sophia and Zelda had was hardly your doing."

"Maybe I feel guilty because of the new card," Declan said. "Like I messed up somewhere."

"You sure you don't want me to walk you home?"

Declan took in the pint-sized woman and shook his head. "If I can't make it the last few blocks, I've got bigger problems."

Maeve reached into her bag and extracted a silver chain. She handed Declan the whistle. "If you get into trouble, blow this."

Declan turned the item over in his hand. "And what, you'll come running?"

"No, you great oaf. It's supposed to startle someone long enough for you to run."

Declan pocketed the gift. "Thanks, Maeve."

Maeve dropped off at her front door, the yapping chorus beckoning from within, and Declan made his way home.

Sturrock had delivered a load of supplies. Stacks of lumber leaned against the house along with two cans of paint.

Declan hesitated, one foot on the lowest ladder rung. Lyncus hung out of the backpack, the raw coffee beans within his booster. Declan tilted his head, taking in the black sky, stars peeking out between the clouds. His eyes fell on the back door of Jess's house. In minutes, he was inside, his phone's flash-light scanning the kitchen cupboards.

At the back of a cabinet, he found a lidded metal pot with a crank on the side. "Borrowing this, Jess. I hope that's okay." He set the device on the counter, knocking over one of several bottles sitting there. Declan stooped to snatch it before it rolled too far in the dark. He shone a flashlight on the label.

"Take at bedtime," he read, and stood, bottle in hand. The label had Jess's name and an Astoria pharmacy's printed in stark black ink. When he set it on the counter near the others, he spotted a sheet of paper anchored down with a bottle. Declan freed the paper from its weight and scanned the note. There was a number followed by several zeros and the initials TK. Below it, someone had calculated two figures. On impulse, Declan pocketed the note.

The rest of the house was still. Declan took the stairs two at a time. At the door of a bedroom, he paused. This one held a large screen television propped up on a dresser. A pair of jeans draped over a chair, a bra lay on its cushion, and a pair of clogs were tucked underneath. There was a romance novel at the bedside, one Declan recognized from Harmonia's collec-tion. The room was an intimate picture of a woman who'd ceased to be. Declan backed out of the room and closed the door.

On the widow's walk, Declan held the railing between his hands, the meal cold against his palm. The sky purpled at the horizon. City lights winked as a mist rolled in. He watched as the night settled.

As was now his custom, he restarted the record player before exiting the house. On his way to the ladder, he sent a text.

"I've got one more favor to ask."

TWENTY-TWO

kunky. The scent of the product from the shop next door wafted in the shop each time their door opened. Declan puttered out in front of the Ram & Rose, clearing the matching whiskey barrel planters of spent summer blooms. Declan planted some bright coleus plants to refresh the contents. At the curb, a white SUV pulled up parallel to the shop.

"Got your list," Anastasia said, climbing out of the car and waving a paper in the air. She wore a woolen scarf wrapped around her neck.

"That was fast," Declan said. "Come inside." He held the door open for her and followed behind. "I've even got coffee."

"From where? That shack where every drink is practically a sugar bomb?"

Declan said, "Better. Or at least, I hope it is. Made it myself."

"You did what now?"

Declan poured the roasted beans into a grinder, flipped a switch, and the machine whirred to life. "Roasted the beans in Jess's popcorn popper. You can find directions for everything on the internet." He poured the grounds into a coffee filter and slid this into the bar's coffee maker. "You'll be my guinea pig. Can't sell donuts without coffee." The machine burbled to life and within moments, a dark liquid dribbled into the carafe.

"True enough," Anastasia said. "Never had artisan brew before." She spread the sheet out on the bar top and took out her phone. "These are all the properties purchased by TurnKey in the last year. There aren't any listings before that."

"So, they're new in town."

Anastasia scrolled on her screen. "Company out of Palo Alto. They specialize in 'upscale living and business environments.'"

"Code for high price." Declan set two mugs near the hot pot of coffee.

"They specialize in waterfront properties, the bulk of them in California."

Declan poured the rich, dark liquid into their mugs. He set one in front of Anastasia alongside a small restaurant pitcher of cream. "Should I just go down the list?"

Some of the street names of TurnKey's purchases were familiar. Commercial. Marine. Duane. Numbered streets made sense, too. He opened the maps app and tapped in an address. "Klatskanine have any good views?"

Anastasia nodded. "Depends on which end, but mostly, yes."

Declan entered another address. "This one is near a park and the school."

"These bottom five are all on a pier," Anastasia said. "Here's Sophia's place."

"We know that one's commercial."

"What I can't figure out"—Anastasia took a sip—"oh, it's not bad! A little...intense, but not bad."

"Thanks," Declan said. He took a sip and grimaced. "Strong."

Anastasia shrugged. "I like my coffee how I like my dates. Never could take that watery filth they brew at work. Tastes like a gas station left the used wiper fluid out overnight in a sandstorm."

Declan slid a plate of mini donuts toward Anastasia. "You were saying?"

She dunked her donut into the hot beverage and took a bite. "Yep. You're right about the coffee. This is my lunch today, by the way." She polished off the donut and brushed her hands together to rid herself of crumbs. "But yes, I'm curious what they did with all the properties."

"Flipped them?" Declan had learned the term from late night television shows. To his understanding, a husband and wife yelled at each other for an hour while others transformed a house into something that never failed to delight its owners while the couple pretended they did it all themselves.

"Possible." She flipped the sheet over and scanned the rest of the list. "We could drive around and check them out."

"We could do that. Or...?"

Anastasia grinned. "Or we investigate my way."

"I'll get my coat."

They stood in the middle of the park, a short distance from the playground equipment. Once in place, Anastasia unpacked the drone, popped in fresh batteries, and checked it over. Declan held the list, serving as the navigator.

"Which one's first?"

"How about 748 Lexington?"

"I'm on it." The drone came to life as its propellers blurred in motion.

Declan watched the camera screen for any signs of interest. Seven forty-eight came into view, the black numbers above the door. A single-story house, unremarkable. Curtains in the windows, a brief front yard of grass and shrubs.

"Wait," Declan said. "Can you go back to the front?" Anastasia worked the controls until the front door was back in view. "There's a lockbox on the door."

"Like it's for sale again?" Anastasia peered at the screen.

"There's no sign out front," Declan said.

Anastasia navigated to the next address, a two-story home with cedar siding on Seventh.

"Another lockbox."

Anastasia stood over his shoulder. "I don't see any signs of people living there. No bikes or potted plants. No paper on the front doorstep or idle trash cans out front."

The other houses revealed a similar pattern. A lockbox or a coded entry, little in the way of personality anywhere to be seen.

Anastasia brought the drone back for a fresh battery. She consulted her phone. "This is interesting."

"What is?" Declan held the drone. He loved the tiny, intricate pieces.

"These are all short-term rentals. Vacation homes."

"Like hotel rooms?"

Anastasia nodded. "Looks like it. I've checked the first five, but I'm guessing the rest are the same."

Declan thought of Ram & Rose filled with beds. "Steve wouldn't have killed Jess just to sell her house—would he?" He thought of the number on the sheet of paper.

"You said they had a date planned. Maybe she canceled it and he freaked out on her."

"Or maybe she was trying to figure out how to afford the restaurant."

"Let's check another few places. I need footage, anyway."

Round two followed the same pattern, including the industrial spots. They'd found a rental in the middle of a city block, the two-bedroom advertising unmatched walkability.

"There are more and more of these," Anastasia said. "My sister claims half of the California coast is now filled with rentals like these."

"Must be big business." On the screen, Declan spotted a familiar figure. "It's Hamilton." The man rolled kegs from the back of the massive brewery to a back loading dock. When he spotted the drone, he picked up a rock and threw it at the tiny aircraft.

"Going to bring her in. This one isn't mine. They'll kill me if I bring back a damaged bird."

As Anastasia changed course, Hamilton said something to someone out of the camera's range and pointed at the drone. Declan said, "Better get it back. This doesn't look good."

A few minutes later, the drone came into sight, angling its way across the field to Anastasia. Behind it, a patrol car slid into the parking lot. Rooney stepped out and crossed the stretch of grass to where they waited.

"You know I've got a license," Anastasia said before the officer could open his mouth. "And I'm on assignment for the city. There's an ad campaign for the Festival of the Dark Arts and they want new footage."

Rooney shifted his jaw. He jerked his chin toward Declan. "Then what's he doing here?"

"He's my friend," Anastasia said.

"I'm interested in becoming a pilot," Declan said.

Anastasia turned to him. "You are?"

"Yeah," Declan said. "I love this stuff."

"You're not concerned about fraternizing at night with someone you barely know—especially someone who might be dangerous?"

"Excuse me," Declan said, heat gathering at his collar. "Are you accusing me of something?"

"Just looking out for a lady. That's more than you did," Rooney said. He turned to Anastasia. "The park closes at dusk. Might be about time to pack up and move on."

"Pssht, it's barely five," Anastasia said. Rooney glared at her. "Besides, the park's empty except for us."

Rooney shook his head and turned back toward his car. "Quit spying, Anastasia Stokes, or I'll let a certain boss know what you're up to on company time. Besides, a broken drone camera fits well in my pocket."

"Jerk," Anastasia said to the retreating car. "Can't believe Jess ever dated that creep."

Twenty-Three

"**A**re you going to tell me who that lady was who stopped by the other day—or not?"

Declan froze in place. He held a tack and one end of a string of lights. Below him, Maeve held the other end, giving him slack as he lined the front of the shop.

"What lady?"

"Oh, come on now," Maeve teased. "You can't tell me that a modern day Audrey Hepburn waltzed in here and you didn't notice."

Declan continued affixing the tacks. One pierced the side of his thumb, and he swore. "Gods!" Declan stuck the injured thumb in his mouth and sucked on it. Thumb still between his teeth, he said, "I don't know who you're talking about."

Maeve draped the light strand around her neck in an exaggerated gesture, popped her hip out, and flicked her hair over her shoulder. "You so do. She was the woman who calls people 'dah-ling' while smoking from a long-handled cigarette."

Declan exhaled. He closed his eyes and winced. "That... was my mother."

"Your...*mother*?"

Declan gave his head a little shake and gritted his teeth. "Everyone has a mother."

"Not everyone has *your* mother," Maeve said under her breath.

"What's that supposed to mean?"

Maeve smiled up at him. "Nothing. Wish I'd got to meet her, that's all."

Declan climbed down from his perch on a stool. "I'm surprised you didn't come over and introduce yourself since you were spying on me. Isn't that what neighbors do in novels about small towns?"

"Astoria's not *that* small. Will she be here for the open house?"

Declan reached for the box of lights and extracted a second rope. "Don't think so."

"Not that type, eh?" Maeve gave him a knowing look.

"She wanted to come. I told her not to," Declan said, then returned to his task. Guilt over shooing her away nagged at him. Should he have been more welcoming? He could have shown her the goodness in his life. Take her to get fish and chips and climb the old tower. Let her meet his friends. Declan chewed at his lower lip.

Maeve was quiet for a few moments, thinking. "I never knew my mom. Wish I had."

Declan rolled his eyes and faced Maeve. "Look, it's not like that. My mother is...overbearing. Oppressive. Thinks she makes better decisions than I do. Inserts herself into every part of my life until she's wound so deeply in the drama it's no longer mine to affect." Declan's face reddened with each descriptor until the heat reached his scalp. "I can't help but think she wants me to fail so she can sweep in and save me from myself once again."

"Sounds about right," Maeve said.

"What?"

Maeve reached for the dangling end of the strand. "I just mean that some mothers are complicated, that's all. What they think is best doesn't always translate."

"Not sure anything she wanted is best for me." Declan tasted his bitterness. Outside a series of honks shook him from his self-pity.

"Do you have any sisters or brothers?"

A gurgling sound signaled the end of the coffee machine's brew cycle. "Couple brothers and a sister." Declan crossed to the little kitchen. He hadn't thought of himself as a child in ages. "Were you ever a...mother?" Declan held his breath, worried he'd overstepped. He carried the two steaming mugs out of the kitchen.

"No." Maeve's voice wavered. She accepted the mug. "It wasn't meant to be." She took a sip. "But I've mother*ed* many. I can relate a little."

Declan draped the last of the lights over an errant nail, the cord dangling down toward the outlet. He plugged in the strand. The shop lit with a soft glow, ringed with light.

"It's perfect," Maeve said.

"I hope it's enough."

"How about you take the numbered streets? Every other ought to do it. I'll take the east-west ones."

"Got it," Pax said. He stuffed the roll of Open House fliers under his arm and slid the stapler into the pocket of his over-sized pants.

"Last one to Dish pays for the ice cream."

"You're on," Pax said. He mounted his skateboard and was off.

Declan started on Marine. He stapled a flier to the first telephone pole. Past the pier, a bald eagle perched on massive scaffolding stretching over a shop. Several pigeons crowded along the lower rung, in awe of their neighbor. As Declan walked, he took in more of the sights. Sea lions barked from rocks. A man rode by on a bicycle, a ferret draped around the back of his neck. Two women walked arm in arm, enjoying ice cream cones. Late afternoon light cast the shops in a warm hue. A breeze teased at Declan's collar.

Declan made his way up the main street before wrapping back north on Commercial. He waved at those he recognized and nodded at those he didn't. For the first time, a sense of belonging crept into his conscience and settled in his heart.

Bernie squatted outside the museum, weeding the side beds. "Declan! What have you got there?"

"Morning." Declan handed her the flier. "I'm having an open house at the shop. I hope you'll come."

Bernie scanned the flier. "You and *both* your neighbors?"

Declan shrugged. "Mudra was a given. When I went next door to tell the fellas, they wanted in on it. I figure it couldn't hurt. Might even get the pawn shop to join in, and the arcade. Maeve's going to ask."

"Mind if I put this up inside?"

"Course not," Declan said. "Pax and I are papering the town with them."

"Paxton Knight?" Bernie looked from the paper to Declan.

"Yeah. He's faster than I am. It's the wheels."

Bernie shook her head. "Hates me, that one, I'm sure of it. His whole family does."

"Why?" Declan could hardly picture Pax hating anyone.

"My father got his grandfather killed."

⁓

They sat at a cramped table jammed in one of the two offices. Bernie poured him a cup of weak tea, offering a packet of sugar. She wedged herself into a metal chair angled into the corner of the room. From a shelf above a narrow desk, she pulled a scrapbook out from between the bookends. While she flipped through the pages, Declan studied the decor. There were awards in frames along the walls. Photographs of Bernie with different people. A scattering of pens across the desktop.

Bernie spun the scrapbook on the surface of the table until it faced Declan. She tapped a picture of two men, arms around each other's shoulders. They stood in front of a cannery, the black-and-white image bleached by a sunny day. "That's my father, Angus, and Pax's grandfather. Co-workers. Fought for worker's rights. Wanted safety at the cannery. More than one of their own had lost a limb or died on the job. Things were different then."

Declan studied the photograph, the easy smile of the men. They wore identical dungarees over dark boots. Pax's grandfather's arm was slung over Angus' shoulders, a wedding band glinting in the light.

"There was unrest. Strikes. This was a dangerous time to work at the factories. The canning industry was changing, owners fighting with all they had. Some of the work shifted overseas and folks fought to maintain profits."

"I read about some of that in the exhibits."

Bernie nodded in approval. "My father wasn't the type to sit back when things got tough. Viking blood in that one. In me, too, I suppose. Angus wouldn't back down, saw through every sneaky trick the owners tried. One night, he snuck over to the cannery. Waited until the night guard stepped out for a smoke break and set a fire. He thought everyone was gone, you see. Had no idea his best mate was in late, replacing a pressure gauge. He'd been on call..." Bernie trailed off, then licked at her lips. "They say the explosion would have made for a quick end."

Declan looked at Bernie. She turned her head. "Dad was never the same after that. Drowned himself in drink until the ghost of his past couldn't reach him.

"Pax's father couldn't handle the grief. He worked for the cannery, too. Quit the day he found out. Became a deep-sea fisherman and was gone for months every year, leaving Pax and his mom alone at home. That boy missed having a father around because mine took things a step too far."

"That is incredibly sad," Declan said. "But you can't be blamed for that." Declan remembered Pax's complaints about his stepfather. He understood how a boy grown used to an absent parent would be resentful and suspicious of a present one.

Bernie nodded and reached for the scrapbook. She re-shelved the volume among the others on the shelf, then downed the last of her tea. "I know. But to a boy who's lost his father, that's a tough thing to explain. My father was different...after. Generations go by before you realize you're entrenched in their stories from the past."

Declan thought of his own absent father, a figurehead at best, his mother overcompensating for the absence. Restless, Declan glanced at the clock ticking away from its post on the wall. "I should go," he said. "Before Pax worries I've reneged on the ice cream."

Bernie stood to make room for Declan to shuffle out of the room. She followed him to the steps. "You're a good man, keeping tabs on that boy."

Declan paused at the door. "Pax is a good kid."

"They all are," Bernie said, nodding. "Sometimes we forget to treat them that way."

TWENTY-FOUR

Beans tumbled against the aluminum popcorn popper. Declan worried over the process, knowing the difference between roasted and burnt was a fine line.

"Knock, knock," Joe called from the shop door. "Class is over, and Maeve said you might need help tonight—and besides, I brought you something."

With potholders, Declan turned off the gas and moved the pot off the heat. He tipped the container over, the dark brown beans spilling into a wide glass bowl. The beans were a rich bronze toffee. *A medium roast.*

The week had flown by. Declan had spent every waking moment planning for the event. This allowed him to ignore the potential loss of his living space and the nagging suspicion that Jess's death was anything but an accident. Sturrock made progress on the stairs, Declan and Anastasia continued their surveys of the rental properties, and Declan snuck into the old house to play opera every night. He picked up coping strategies from his friends, letting some problems simmer at the back of his mind.

"Nearly ready," Declan said. "Come on in!"

Joe bustled into the small kitchen, filling the doorway. "Smells like heaven."

"I'm about to grind it up," Declan said. "I've been experimenting."

"Well, now you've got some extra play money to fund your trials." Joe extracted a folded paper from within his pocket. "Brought your first paycheck."

"My first paycheck," Declan said. "This deserves a little celebration." He nudged his chin toward a plate of mini donuts before wiping his hands on his apron and then accepting the check.

Joe selected one ring of cake and took a bite. "Strawberry... and...pistachio?"

Declan nodded. "Red—well, pink—and green. Planning to reopen the donut window for the holidays. Seeing if I can put together a menu ahead of time. Don't think my little advice column is going to pay the big bills."

Joe put a heavy hand on Declan's shoulder. "Glad you plan to stay, my friend. Wasn't too sure about that."

"Oh?" Declan put the filter on a scale and measured out the grounds.

Joe leaned against the doorjamb. The smooth skin on his cheek was pink, as though freshly shaved. "Me and Cate took bets, you see, as to how long someone like you could last."

Declan turned to face Joe, an eyebrow raised. "Who won?"

"Neither of us," Joe said, sheepish. "And I'm happy we lost."

Declan assembled a tray of mugs while he considered Joe's revelation. "Then I am, too." With his own vulnerabilities at play, Declan took a risk. "We're friends, then, Joe?"

"Undoubtedly," Joe said, and whacked Declan on the back.

Declan all but dropped the tray, the mugs rattling.

"Sorry, mate. Don't know my own strength." Joe reached to steady the tray.

"Don't worry about it," Declan said. He didn't want to lose the bulk of his remaining restaurant mugs. "Would you bring the donuts?"

Maeve hurried in from next door. "Studio lights are on, granola bar samples are out, and I've got music playing." She took in the room. "This place looks great!" Maeve walked over to the pair of deep log chairs near the window under one of the remaining restaurant lighting fixtures.

"The trees that needed thinning—for fire safety," Joe said.

Cate had dropped off some netting that morning. The brown rope lattice made a great backdrop on which to hang a selection of air plants. Anastasia had printed some of her best drone shots of foliage and Declan had those printed in black and white on giant canvases that now lined the long wall. Sturrock's potting stand was paired with a bench from the old restaurant giving Declan a terrarium building station. The place was more than a shop, it was an experience.

Declan had left Lyncus at home. Having a cat underfoot among the public seemed risky. For his part, the feline ignored the plate of cat food Declan offered and pouted by the window.

"That's an unusual decoration," Maeve said. She faced the bar, staring up at the wall.

Above the mirror, Declan had placed the last two artifacts of his former life. Two arrows, one gold, one silver, made an X against the wall.

"I like it," Joe said. "Gives this place real hunter-gatherer vibes. Natural-like."

"Thanks," Declan said, avoiding Maeve's gaze.

"And are these...roses?" To Declan's relief, Maeve had turned away from the bar. She stood in front of the cooler case, her fingertips pressed to the glass.

"I just cleaned that," Declan said, wiping at the fingerprints.

"So," Maeve said. "Roses?"

Declan shrugged, staring at the long-stemmed beauties in the case, their rainbow of color a careful arrangement. "I still think they are overdone, but..." Declan trailed off. He thought of the silent suffering, the shy crushes, and the tributes to great love. "I think symbols are important, too. Sometimes they communicate in ways that words cannot."

"I'll take a dozen," Joe said, his eyes on the flowers.

"Oh...uh, of course." Declan reached for his apron. He'd had it embroidered with a new shop logo. "Which colors would you like—or is this a gift?"

"It's a...well. I'm giving it to someone. Someone I admire. But nothing serious. A friend. Who's a girl, but not a girlfriend. I want to give it to her tonight, after the party."

"You'd like to give a woman flowers. That's lovely," Maeve said, assuring Joe with a pat on his arm. "How about a mix of colors?"

Joe nodded at her suggestion, relieved to be free of some of the pressure, and Maeve shot Declan a look.

Declan took over. "How about some reds and oranges—and a little pink? Gives off the look of a sunset."

"Beautiful," Maeve said, as Declan reached for the flowers.

"In fact," Declan said, "if it's okay with you, I'll keep the bouquet in here until you're ready to take it. That way, everyone can see it. I've got a vase and everything." He got to work on the arrangement.

Joe took a deep breath. "Thanks, guys."

"Want to open the doors?" Declan attempted to maintain an even voice while butterflies beat a pattern in his stomach. One or two customers he could handle, and a lack of any he could complain about.

An hour in, and the shop was stuffed to the gills with people.

"Pax, are you good to run the machine? I've got more batter in the fridge, labels on the bowls." Declan dumped the spent grounds into the compost and replaced them with a fresh batch.

"Got it down," the boy said. "We'll have butternut caramel beauties in minutes. Do they get a glaze?"

"Yes, the coffee drizzle and a sprinkle of crushed hazelnuts."

"Aye aye, Captain." He picked up one of the rings, fresh from the machine. "Say, do these look anything like—"

"Don't even think about saying it!" Declan rushed back out to the shop. He sidled up to Joe. The man held court over a trio of women at the terrarium booth.

"You'll want to choose a couple of plants, one from the shorter variety and one that will give a little height. This creates visual interest, like in a forest." With deft chopsticks, Joe helped a woman disentangle a *Fittonia* for her selection.

"Need anything here?" Declan asked.

Joe held up one woman's creation. "Yolanda put this together. Isn't it stunning?"

"Are you the owner?" This came from a woman with dark eyes rimmed in thick lashes. She removed one of the Ram & Rose aprons and hung it on the wall hooks near the table. Joe handed her the small glass vessel, another thrift store find. "This was too much fun. I hope you consider running another class! I could use another one of these for my office."

Declan hadn't anticipated the popularity of the table. "That's a great idea. I'll see what I can put together."

"I dropped my number on your mailing list," Yolanda said, shifting her gaze to the register where Anastasia stood, ringing up purchases. The woman stepped closer to Declan.

He smelled lavender and oranges. She blinked up at him. "Call me anytime. Day or night." With a wink, she took her purchase from Joe and sashayed out of the shop, hips swishing.

Joe stood at Declan's side as the two watched her leave the shop. She gave Declan a little wave through the window. "Does that happen...often?" Joe asked.

In the past couple of weeks, Declan hadn't seen many people beyond his friends and the occasional customer. Still, everyone from the letter carrier to the grocery checkout clerks lingered over their time with him, offering everything from their phone numbers to a proposal of marriage from a German tourist. *Thanks, Mom.* "Eh..." he said, to downplay the attention. "I'm an exotic outsider, that's all."

"Here I'd always considered myself as a guy from the fringes. Guess I'm a bit too local for that." Joe scratched at a spot on his upper arm.

Declan turned to Joe with a sudden curiosity. Not once had the man gushed over him, flirted, or offered so much as a suggestive wink. "Joe—don't take this anywhere beyond the basic question—but do you think I'm an attractive guy?"

Joe tilted his head to consider Declan. "Sure. I mean, you've got that golden skin thing going on, which is pretty cool. Complements your eyes. And not every guy can pull off curls, which you totally do. I wish my hair did that." Chin in hand, Joe squinted at Declan, studying him further. "Your nose is a little small. Pert, I think, is the term. You've got decent lips, but I think one ear is slightly higher than the other." Declan frowned, unused to the scrutiny. "But, yeah. I'd say as far as dudes go, you're a looker. I ought to get some product suggestions from you. The season's wreaking havoc on my skin." Joe scratched at his arm again. "It's this new wax they're using. I don't think it's gentle stuff."

An officer strolled into the shop, and Declan gulped. This

was the same one Declan saw with Rooney that morning outside the Pastry House. The urge to hide squeezed his lungs and he did his best to shrug it off. When the man spotted Declan, he hurried over.

Declan closed his eyes, willing himself to sink through the floor and out of sight. This was the moment he would be evicted, forced to leave because a new owner found a loophole.

"Good evening, officer. What can I do for you?"

"Word on the street is you're the man to see about a donut."

Declan's mouth stretched into a nervous grin. "Guilty as charged," he said, and winced. "Come on in."

"I'm the new guy on the force and drew the short straw for this event, but I'm loving this community you've got here. This place is really hopping!" The officer made a beeline for the food. He chose an apple donut, sprinkled with cinnamon sugar. "Just signed up for some yoga next door. Doc says I have to do something about my blood pressure."

While Maeve taught mini yoga classes throughout the night, Cate commanded the reception desk, registering new students and selling coconut water. The owners of Going Green had a host of giveaways, too, but he guessed the officer wouldn't be visiting that shop.

"Smart choice," Declan said, eyeing the man as he reached for a second donut. "You'll love them. Maeve's great."

The man made a face. "Do you think I have to put on that *span-dex* everyone always wears? Not sure anyone wants to see me poured into that."

Declan smiled. "Wear what makes *you* comfortable," he said. "Maeve would ask nothing else."

"Declan?" Anastasia called from the register. "Got any more boxes? I'm running low."

The officer touched the tip of his hat with a finger in a salute before selecting another donut from the trays.

"I'll get some—need anything else?" Declan stood next to Anastasia as she rang up a Peperomia in a pot that said *Rooting for You* on the side. The customer, a pregnant woman towing a toddler, gave Anastasia her driver's license and then her medical insurance card as she stared at Declan. When Anastasia again asked the woman for payment, an edge of impatience clipping her request, Declan stepped away from the transaction, allowing the flustered woman to make sense of the contents of her wallet.

Behind him, he heard the woman ask Anastasia if he was single, to which his friend replied, "He is, but from the looks of things, you aren't." Declan snorted as he passed the kitchen, Pax giving him a thumbs up as he waved an icing bottle over a fresh plate of donuts, striping them with chocolate sauce.

Declan headed for the alleyway, an artery in from the street that allowed for backdoor deliveries and trash bin storage. Blessed with a pair of dry days, he'd collected boxes from the other businesses who were all too happy to have him take over their recycling for the event.

Down the alley, Declan nestled smaller boxes within larger ones, like the troika dolls that fascinated him in the thrift shop. Each doll had a smaller version within, the set a family of sorts. He considered his new friends this way, starting with the tiny and charismatic Maeve to the massive and kind Joe. Each was unique, yet they fit together as a set.

Declan stooped to pick up a flattened box when he heard voices at the end of the alley.

"You promised me forty, and I ain't settling for less."

"That was before we had competition," a second voice growled, low and menacing. "You had one job. Get the info before anyone else. Anything less isn't worth forty. Hell, it'll be worth nothing if we lose that house."

"Why do you care so much about that place? There's dozens more of them here, ripe for the picking. Widows, bankruptcy...you know who's about to go belly up before they do. That's the beauty of your job."

"I told you, the client wants the property for the view. They'll tear the place down and build an apartment building."

"She would've hated that."

"Stick to the plan. Get in there and keep him busy. I've got to get that note."

"I'll do my part if you stick to the deal. I open my own place. You head south on that brand-new boat, and we never see each other again."

"I'll text you when it's done."

A car door shut and the car drove off. Declan counted down from a hundred before slipping back into the alleyway and hurrying toward the Ram & Rose.

Twenty-Five

I nside Ram & Rose, a speaker pumped eighties music from behind the bar. Joe's table was overflowing, and Anastasia had a line four deep. Pax brushed past Declan. "We're almost out of chocolate, but I've got more vanilla and chai on the way."

Boxes in hand, Declan took in the sight. His shop was full. In every nook, customers filled the space. They unhooked hanging plants from the stand, consulted tags, and compared colors. His flower fridge was almost empty, with all bouquets sold and only a few single stems left. The net of air plants was almost empty, and he could see shelf space all around the shop. He would have to put in a new order tomorrow. The prospect of a business—a surviving enterprise—made him giddy.

"Excuse me," said a woman with short dark hair. "Are you Declan?"

"I am," Declan said, taking in her cream-colored dress and the man similarly committed to wearing neutral colors who stood silent by her side. He had the perma-smile of someone so accustomed to the expression they struggled to affect any other. The man had one hand at the small of the woman's back.

"I'm Evelyn Ashford, Pax's mom?"

"Oh yes, you're a wonderful baker. Thank you for all the treats!"

The woman looked down and slid the toe of her flat against the floor. "Thank you, you're too kind. It's just a hobby."

"Isn't she amazing?" the man beamed. He held out a spray-tanned hand to Declan, a gold wedding band glinting against his skin. "Tim Ashford. I'm always telling her she ought to get a booth at the Farmer's Market."

Declan nodded. "I agree."

Evelyn's cheeks pinked at the compliments. "You're too kind, but I came to talk about Pax."

Declan blanched. "Is something wrong?"

"No, no," Tim said. "Quite the opposite."

"We wanted to thank you," Evelyn said. "He never wanted to bake with me before and was always out with his friends. I thought, we all grieve in our own ways..." Evelyn faded off and Tim put his arm around his wife and gave her a squeeze. "But now, he's different. He wants to practice his recipes with me, and he's got a new group of friends—"

"A better one," Tim added.

Evelyn nodded. "You've given him somewhere to hang out that's safe. Encouraged him to be a better person. He's acting like a kid again, instead of a grouchy teen. I—we—just wanted to thank you."

A tear perched at the corner of Declan's eye, threatening to fall. The receipt of a compliment that had nothing to do with his looks or power was a novel experience. "I...don't know what to say. He's a great kid."

Tim clapped Declan on the back. "How about you help me pick out some flowers for my lovely wife?"

Declan ushered the couple to the cooler, eager to display the options. Maybe Pax was right that flowers were an important way to send love. If they became a stale habit, that said more about the relationship at hand rather than the gesture. He introduced them to Anastasia at the register, who gushed over Pax.

Hamilton appeared at the shop door, his shifty eyes casing the store. The reminder of what he'd overheard in the alley flooded Declan's brain.

Declan whispered to Anastasia. "Did you get set up—all the way up?"

Anastasia nudged her chin toward a shelf above the bar. Declan flicked his gaze toward the small black box and then back to the brewer.

Hamilton wandered between a few tables until he spotted Declan. Then he feigned interest in a bird fern that bushed out from a tall plant stand.

Declan approached, willing his voice to stay calm. He had too many questions about what he overheard in the alley to be sure about any of it. Best thing to do was ask questions and listen. "Hello there," he said. "Succulents doing okay? Looking for something for the brewery or your place?"

"No. I mean, yes. Well, maybe." Hamilton stumbled over his own words. "What can you tell me about these plants?" He gestured to the pair of ponytail palms filling their pots.

"Can't be left outside," Declan said, hooking one of the curled leaves on a finger. "Not here, anyway. Some in the summer, sure. Pretty easy care, slow growing for us. They like a tight pot and to dry out between watering."

"And, uh...what about these?" Hamilton pointed at a trio of staghorn ferns mounted to cedar planks. "You've got them on those fancy hangers on that ceiling board. That necessary?"

Declan blinked, his lips pursed. "If you were half the

realtor you should have been, you would know that's called crown molding. It's been around since the pharaohs, after all."

Hamilton narrowed his eyes, his lighthearted inquiry turned dark. "What did you say?"

"I'm just thinking that a proper realtor needs to understand selling points. It makes sense that you fall short."

Hamilton's mouth formed a wide circle, then he spluttered like a struggling engine. "But how did you? But I...that's not fair!"

"You're saying Coastal should have kept you even though you were terrible at your job? Dangerous, too, from what I heard."

"That *bastard*," Hamilton spat. "If he wasn't dead, I'd kill him!"

"Wasn't Steve who told me."

Hamilton's face purpled in rage, bright splotches coloring his cheeks. He jabbed a finger at Declan's chest. "Listen here, *pretty boy*." At this, Anastasia looked up from the register and Joe abandoned the terrarium table to move closer. "That prick killed my career before it could start. But you know what? I'm better off. Got a career people love me for. About to open my own place. I'm moving up in the world, while my old buddy Steve went swimming with the sea lions."

Anastasia balked. "How do you know that?"

"Know what?"

"That he was in the river," Anastasia said. "The report said he drowned but didn't say where. Steve used to swim in Coffenbury Lake, not the Columbia."

"Just an expression," Hamilton said, as his face paled. A queasy look took over.

"What I don't understand," Declan said, "is why, if you hate him so much, you two went fishing just the other week."

The rage returned. "What are you talking about?"

"The picture at Storia. Seems strange that three enemies would go fishing together."

"We were *not* friends."

"Fishing buddies, then, is that what you call it? Anyway, what I can't figure out is how you did it."

Hamilton shoved a glass dish full of succulents to the floor where it smashed into little pieces, the plants rolling out over the sand. "Enough!"

Declan held up both hands. "I'm just stating facts. Last time I checked it isn't a crime to go fishing, but it sure is to murder someone."

"Is there a problem here?" Gone was the cheerful, donut-chomping officer. Instead, the man rested his palms on his belt, ready.

"I've got evidence that this man knows what happened to Steve Corey. And I think he knows something about Jessica Black as well."

"I never touched her!" Hamilton shrieked. Dozens of conversations stopped, their eyes all on Hamilton.

"But you did hurt Steve?"

"That's not what I said!"

"We've got footage of what you've been up to—casing houses and reporting them back to your employer," Declan said. "Can get that to you anytime, Officer..." Declan read the name on the man's uniform. "Blossom. In the meantime, he did this to my shop." Declan pointed to the broken glass, then turned back to Hamilton. "Pretty sure he can arrest you for trashing my store."

The officer removed his handcuffs from his belt. "Sir, have you had anything to drink tonight?"

"Of course I have, I work in a brewery. Doesn't mean I'm drunk. And you can't arrest me based on what he said," Hamilton said. He backed up toward the exit. "It's his word against mine,"

"We all saw you do it," Anastasia said.

"Officer Blossom," the official said. "And yes, I can."

"But I didn't—" Hamilton looked from the officer, to Anastasia, to Declan, and turned to run for the door. He collided with the broad chest of Joe Pavlovich. Joe grabbed the smaller man by the shoulders in a bear hug.

The officer secured one of Hamilton's wrists before grabbing the other. "Hamilton Wainwright, you are under arrest for criminal mischief and the destruction of property. You have the right to remain silent. Anything you say..." The officer continued as he maneuvered Hamilton out the front door.

"I want a lawyer," Hamilton shouted over the hushed whispers. "A good one!"

When they'd gone, Anastasia mounted on her knees on top of a stool and addressed the crowd. "Sorry about that, folks. Now that the trash is out, let's get back to it, shall we? There's only a half hour left, and I see a table full of button ferns looking for new plant parents."

The crowd returned to life, the recent events on everyone's lips. Declan made a quick sweep of the floor, then hurried to restock where he could, taking orders where he couldn't. Those at the craft table finished their projects and scurried out into the night. Pax delivered the last of the donuts—maple bacon—to the remaining customers before busying himself at the dishwasher. When Anastasia processed the last payment and Declan locked the door, the four of them collapsed onto the stools. Maeve and Cate had already gone home, exhausted by the evening.

Anastasia pressed the cashbox into Declan's hands. "Didn't count it, but since it was just me, if it's wrong, you know where to find this cashier. Going home to soak my feet." She slipped into her coat and patted her pockets to find her keys. Declan reached up to snag the drone camera from its perch and handed it to her. "I'll get this footage to Officer Blossom in the morning," she said. "Good job getting him on recording."

"And all I'd wanted was some content for advertising. Practically got a full confession of murder instead."

Anastasia smiled as she pocketed the device. "G'night, friends. Let's do this again...next year."

When she was halfway out the door, Declan let out a low whistle to Joe. The burly man had been watching Anastasia's departure with longing. Declan pointed to the bouquet, the lone item remaining in the cold case. A tall "Not for Sale" card nestled among the blooms. "*Go*," Declan mouthed.

Joe hefted the bouquet in his arms and hustled out the door, the top half swinging open in his wake.

Pax rolled his eyes. "Is it always like this?"

"What's that?" Declan stared out the window, a smile on his face. They'd all suspected Joe's crush on Anastasia.

"All this love stuff." Pax made a face.

Declan attempted to sound nonchalant while his insides melted. There'd been perks to his old job, and moments like this were among them. "Why are you asking me?"

"Aren't you the expert?"

This is it, Declan told himself. *The moment I'm found out, exposed. I'll be on the next damn train to Olympus.*

"I just write a column in the local paper," Declan said, and shrugged. "What do I know?"

Pax scratched at the back of his head. "Adults must have a lot of problems if they need someone else to mind their business."

"Eh, when you get older, that's a lot of how you show you care for other people. You can only give someone so many pairs of socks. People show their love by wanting to help. Even if they don't always go about it the right way. Like your stepdad."

"Yeah," Pax said. He took a deep breath and let it out. "Did I tell you he got a new job?"

"Oh, really?"

"He quit that big company. Said they were filling cities with garbage homes and charging a fortune for them. He works for the Parks department now. Said he wanted to make more places for kids like me to go."

"That's great news."

Pax retrieved his skateboard from behind the sales counter. "I'll be back by tomorrow."

"I'll have your money ready."

"Any chance I can experiment with some new flavors?"

Declan smiled. "Anytime."

TWENTY-SIX

Declan finished vacuuming shards of glass from every corner of the room. He'd debated waiting until morning, sleepiness dragging his pace, but figured he should at least get a start on the cleanup. The whirring of the vacuum became white noise against which his thoughts wandered.

They'd nabbed Hamilton for the murder of Steve Corey, and that was a triumph. The man all but admitted he'd been the one to drown Steve—but how? The why was fuzzy, too. Revenge for a decade-old snub seemed too severe at best. None of this brought them closer to finding out what happened to Jess. He turned off the machine, fatigue winning the battle over the shop's cleanliness.

"Mr. Rosewood."

Declan jumped. He turned to find Rooney hanging over the lower half of the split door. The man had a scratch on his jaw, an angry red line.

"You shouldn't creep up on a guy like that," Declan said.

"I'm told we have you to thank for the arrest of one Hamilton Wainwright. Possible suspect for the murders of

Steve Corey and Jessica Black." The officer patted his palms on the door. "Okay if I come in?"

"Sure," Declan said, annoyed at the intrusion. "I'm almost done, though, then I'm headed home. Long day and all." Declan busied himself with putting the cashbox in his bag, turning off the warmer on the coffee machine, and unplugging the string of fairy lights.

Rooney stepped inside and let his gaze roam the interior. "Must have been a successful night," he said. "This place used to be full of plants" The man paused at the bar, scrutinizing the set-up.

"Anastasia took it with her," Declan said, "if you're looking for the camera. She's sending over footage in the morning."

"Of course, of course," Rooney said. "She's so...observant, that one."

"Well, I'd love to stay and chat, but I'm going to lock up instead. So, if you don't mind..." Declan held his hand out in front of the open door in suggestion.

"Great place," Rooney said again, giving the shop one last look. "Hoping you get to keep it."

"Why wouldn't I? Despite the drama, tonight was just what I needed. Should be okay for a while yet. Not enough to buy a boat or anything big like that, but...say, do you fish?" Declan turned to measure Rooney's expression, but the man's face was shadowed.

"Most folks around here fish." Rooney stood by his car, street side. "Why?"

"Thought I saw a picture of you on a fishing trip with some others. Wasn't sure it was you, so I asked the owner of the guide outfit. See, he's my friend's ex—"

Rooney's face darkened. He pasted on a smile. "Say, how about I give you a ride? I know you don't drive, after all. Couldn't find a license in the system."

Declan's eyes widened for a moment before he returned Rooney's grin. In a cheerful tone, he replied, "Why would I need to drive? I don't have a car."

Rooney said, "Easy enough to manage when those of us with vehicles are happy to give you a lift. Come on, get in."

Declan hesitated. If he didn't take the ride, Rooney could follow him on foot or by car. If he accepted the ride, this interaction would end earlier.

Declan eased into the passenger's seat. When he reached for the seat belt, something jabbed him under his fingernail. "Ouch!" He extracted a gold hoop wedged between the seatbelt and the seat, its post having just stuck into him. He held it up for Rooney. "Missing something?"

Rooney flinched, a subtle contraction of the muscles along his cheek. "Must belong to one of the perps," Rooney said. He lifted the lid from a paper coffee cup. "Toss it in here. I'll take care of it."

Declan held onto the earring, looking at it. "Reminds me of the one Jess lost. She was looking for it the day before she died. I wonder how long DNA can live on metal..."

Rooney's eyes flashed in the rearview mirror. "So what if it could have been hers. We dated—everyone knows that. Gave her more than one ride home when she was tipsy. Could have left it in here one of those nights she couldn't see straight."

"Didn't seem wasted the last time I saw her," Declan said. "How about you?"

The officer's eyes widened before he was able to regain control over his reaction. He eased the car away from the curb. "I was on duty the night she died. Storia had a special event. A tap takeover and the premier of their flagship distilled liquors. I stuck close all night in case things got wild. People make dumb decisions, getting behind the wheel."

"Must have been tiring to circle the block." Declan stared out the window as Rooney headed east past the brewery, scanning the back loading dock as if by habit, then turned north toward Jess's house.

"You know," the officer started. "A lot of people want to live here."

"Oh?" Declan said. He willed the few remaining blocks to fly by.

Rooney nodded. "Sure do. People are paying top dollar for housing now. You can understand that, living in one of the classics. Great bones, classic lines—high value to those who want to stand out." Declan said nothing, and Rooney continued. "Some say we should push back. That we shouldn't share the wealth and beauty of this place with outsiders. I disagree."

"You do?" The more Declan kept Rooney talking, the less he'd have to say.

"I think there's room for all of us. If someone doesn't like change, they can leave. I mean, you're new here. Where did you come from, again?"

"Olympia," Declan said.

"Yes, that's right. People like me who are perfectly happy to have people like you move here and make it your own have a right to benefit from that arrangement." Rooney slid the patrol car into Jess's driveway.

"How so?"

"This house," Rooney said, gesturing. "Say someone knew of someone else looking to buy. There's nothing wrong with connecting them to a willing seller."

"A willing seller, sure." Declan glanced at the officer.

"And there's nothing wrong with all parties benefiting from that situation, right?"

Declan spotted Lyncus, waiting near the ladder, his eyes glowing in the headlights. A rick rack edge of stairs was nailed to the wall. On the side of the garage, Sturrock had stacked cut pieces of lumber. "I suppose not," he said.

Rooney fished in his chest pocket. "Then why, Declan

Rosewood from Olympia, would you have held onto this?" Rooney unfolded the sheet of notepaper, covered in figures.

"That's not mine," Declan said with a smile, his hands sweaty against his slacks.

"Oh, I know that. It's my own handwriting, and my mistake to leave it out where a snoop could find it. A smart man would have used it as leverage. Tried to get in on the deal. A smart man wouldn't have left it up in his apartment where anyone could find it. But you aren't a smart man, are you, Mr. Rosewood?"

Adrenaline streamed through his body in the debate between fight or flight. He was strong, yes, but in a human body stuck in a car with a man in possession of a gun. "I don't know what you're talking about. You've got your paper now. How about I go inside and we forget all about this situation."

"Save your act for the ladies." The officer grabbed a lighter from the dash and flicked the red switch. He held the tiny flame to the corner of the paper. "Wouldn't want this information in the wrong hands."

Declan used the distraction to wrench the door open and dive out of the car.

"Dammit!" Rooney yelled behind him.

Declan stumbled to his feet, then ran for the side of the house, seeking an escape route. He could vault a wall, but then what? If Rooney got him in his sights, Declan was a dead man. Footfalls pounded behind him. Declan was fit, but Rooney was keeping up. Declan ducked behind the garage.

"Stop!" Rooney bellowed.

The officer bolted for the side of the building. When he rounded the garage, Declan lifted the ladder. Rooney's shins smacked into the metal rungs, sending the officer sprawling across the concrete.

TWENTY-SEVEN

Rooney sat in the back of a patrol car, his face streaked with blood.

"That's a nasty road rash on a nasty man," Bernie said. She'd seen the red and blue lights and hustled over like a moth to a flame.

When she arrived, Declan sat against the garage, Lyncus in his lap. He stroked the cat, an absentminded movement. Bernie stood before him, giving a play-by-play of the hubbub.

"Newspaper guy—"

"Joe?"

"Yeah, the big one. He's here now. Talking to the portly officer. The one with the soft gray eyes—"

"Blossom."

"Sure, sure, it's him. They're having a chat while that scumbag stews in the back of a car. If he glares any harder, his head's going to explode. Oh wait, another patrol car is rolling up." Bernie's tone shifted. "Ooh and there's that busybody, Masha. Of course, she wouldn't stay in her house and wait for the emergency to be over."

Declan neglected to point out that Bernie, by that definition, was guilty of that exact act.

"And look, she's brought Trish from down the block," Bernie said. "Bet they envy my access, but don't you worry, I won't be telling a soul what I saw. Can't say that about Joe, though. You know how reporter-types are. He's coming this way."

Joe's towering figure loomed over Declan. "Are you going to make it? Word is you refused services."

"I'm a little banged up, that's all," Declan said. "No need for the fuss." In truth, he feared what they'd find if he let the well-meaning people in uniforms poke and prod him with their machines.

"Thought you'd want to know, Blossom says it all checks out. Your story."

Declan smirked. "It's not like I'd make it up."

"Tell me," said Bernie. "Give an old lady a bone to chew."

"TurnKey officials took his call. They named Steve as their guy. They hired him through Coastal to hunt for upcoming investments and get them early access. Steve paid Rooney cash on the side to let him know which properties were likely to hit the market, then gave that information to TurnKey, brokering the deals."

"Slime," Bernie said. "Bottom feeder! I wondered why Katie's house went so quick. Lost her husband to his own sadness, poor man. Moved to Albuquerque to be with her kids. House never had a For Sale sign yet was turned into a nursing home within a month."

Declan nodded. "Anastasia and I went through a list of TurnKey properties. What didn't turn into a fancy rental became high density, upscale housing."

Joe rubbed at his beard. "When Rooney saw dollar signs, he got greedy. That's the loot motivation, right?"

"Sure is," Declan said.

Joe continued. "Hamilton fessed up, too. He always hated Steve. When Rooney promised him enough money to bankroll his own brewery, Hamilton jumped at the chance to get rid of Steve. They took him out fishing like everything was copacetic. Hamilton said Rooney dosed Steve with something—"

"Zolpidem," Declan said.

Joe paused. "Wait, that's what Blossom guessed. How did you know?"

"Saw a bottle on Jess's counter."

Joe nodded as the pieces fit together in his mind. "Well, anyway, they left Steve on the boat. Hamilton came back after dark and rolled the man right into the water. Said he barely made a splash."

Declan allowed for a slow start. His body ached everywhere. When he'd hit the ground, shoulder, hip, and knee collided with hard-packed dirt. The next morning they were tender, throbbing. His wounds itched in the shower, bruises and cuts covering his skin.

He'd opened the store as planned, yet the shop remained empty. He took inventory and rearranged the plants, making a list of what to buy. The quiet of the shop crowded his thoughts.

Pax stopped by as promised, whipping up a batch of Black Forest donuts dipped in a cherry glaze. Declan paid him for both his help at the opening and the recipe.

"Better get going," Pax said when the dishes were clean. "Tim's taking me fishing."

Lyncus hadn't left Declan's side since his dramatic escape from Rooney's car. The cat sat on Declan's lap as he opened the cash box and consulted the screen of sales. He counted the till once and then again. When the numbers flashed again across the screen, Declan blinked.

There, in black and white, was a profit.

"We've done it, Lyncus," he said. The cat swished his tail and nudged the underside of Declan's chin

Declan patted the cat before setting him on the bar. He dug into a cabinet and withdrew a wrapped package, the papers loosely rebound with used tape. He removed the wrapping to reveal a silver frame, a message in script along the bottom.

My angel, I'm so proud of you. Here's to many more. Love, Mom

Declan opened the back of the frame, chose a bill from the neat pile he'd counted, and slid it beneath the glass. He leaned the frame against the bar mirror, just below the arrows, and stood back to admire the effect.

"Greedy scum!" Cate shook her head in disbelief. "And all for a boat!"

"A boat?" Maeve selected a wedge of pita and used it to scoop up a dollop of hummus.

Cate crossed her arms. "That's what the boys said. Rooney was strutting up and down the docks like a sea-born rooster, going on and on about how he'd be picking out a new retirement rig this time next year."

"And what about Jess?"

"Blossom said they'd reopen the case. I expect a host of investigators crawling about the place within days. Fingerprints and reconstruction of the crime scene."

Cate pressed her lips together. "Do you think it will be enough?"

"Anastasia's camera caught Rooney breaking into my place to take the note."

"We did get pretty epic footage of Lyncus attacking Rooney," Anastasia said. "Landed a scratch along his jaw. I'd post it on the internet if it wasn't evidence."

"I'd pay to see that," Joe said.

"They'll find Rooney's fingerprints everywhere, including on the bottle in Jess's house," Declan said. He sipped from his water bottle. "Before he could have claimed they'd dated so his prints all over would make sense. But there was no reason for him to be in my apartment."

"The threads are unraveling," Maeve said. "Good."

"Blossom warned me not to go anywhere, though," Declan said. "Said they'll want to talk to me some more even if Hamilton decides to plea and turn on Rooney."

"No one likes the idea of a corrupt cop." Joe scooped some walnuts from the dish. He crunched as he spoke. "This'll hit the Portland papers, I'm sure of it."

"Poor Jess," Cate said.

"May she rest in peace, now," Anastasia added.

"To Jess," Maeve said, lifting her water bottle. "And justice."

The group was silent, letting the residual sadness settle. Declan unfolded his legs and stood. "I'd like to say something."

"Please do," Maeve said.

"I wanted to thank you all," Declan said. "For everything you did for me. Last night was a raging success—because of you." He paused, swallowing. "I am a success because of you."

Cate smiled. Joe wiped away a tear with one of his massive fingers. Anastasia hugged her knees, watching him. Maeve stood to fill his bottle.

"I'm a better person now," Declan said. His voice faltered as his own tears threatened to breach. "And I..." He trailed off, then raised his water bottle. "To you all." The group echoed his gesture.

"We've got a new card," Cate said brightly, blinking away her tears.

"Well, let's have it," Maeve said. "Bleeding Hearts, come to order."

~

Maeve settled the hood of her rain jacket over her head. The faint drizzle pattered at the rooftops and sent rivulets down the sidewalk. "How are you holding up?" she asked.

"Okay," Declan said, at her side. "Good, mostly. It's just been...well...a lot. Unexpected. I'm not used to this much... emotion."

"I'd love to tell you this is the last of it," Maeve said. She hoisted her yoga bag farther up her shoulder. "But hearts are made of muscle, not bone. They get stronger through hard work, never shortcuts."

"Yeah," Declan said. "I guess I'd grown far too used to shortcuts."

"Life is tough. Love and get hurt. Don't risk your heart and get hurt, anyway. Being human is mostly bouncing back from pain in the best ways you can."

When they reached Maeve's fence line, she faced Declan. "I've been debating whether to say anything."

"Say anything about what?"

The dogs began the nightly bark. Several pairs of beady eyes appeared in the window.

"Have you...kept anything? From your past life."

Declan looked at Maeve. She avoided his gaze. "What do you mean?"

"You know—any of the good parts."

Declan frowned at the woman. "I don't understand."

Maeve snagged a leaf from the maple arching over their heads. "When you reach a certain age, all of us have baggage. A past. We hide these things from others, shoving them to the back of our personalities, not wanting to explain to anyone that side we've left behind. But these parts of us are still there, waiting for the time we may need them again."

Maeve held the leaf out, her eyes locked on its surface. First it turned golden, then orange, then bright crimson. When Maeve looked up, her eyes glowed with a soft green light. She placed the red leaf in his hand. "It's okay to be you, still. In whatever way makes sense. At least in front of me."

Declan stared at the leaf on his palm, the crisp edges curled. Memories flooded his brain as he struggled to take hold of his emotions.

"I'll be right back. Don't go anywhere." Maeve hurried up the front walk. She unlocked the door and entered to a chorus of greetings. The porch light flipped on, then the lamp in the living room. In minutes, she descended the front steps, holding something behind her back. "I've shown you a piece of my past. You might think I'd ask for a piece of yours in return."

Declan had considered as much as he'd held the leaf, but said nothing.

"It would be the custom, I know this," Maeve said. "If I didn't already have something."

From behind her back, she withdrew an object wrapped in a raw silk scarf and handed it to Declan. When he accepted the bulk, he knew instantly what he held.

"How did you...but...how can I...?" he asked, as tears striped his cheeks. "Maeve, I—"

She smiled and reached out to squeeze his arm. "You don't need to say anything," she said. "But if you're up for it, I'd love to hear a song."

Declan took the ladder rungs, two at a time. Once inside his apartment, he set his lute, once again wrapped in Maeve's scarf, atop the table.

After offering Lyncus a pungent can of tuna recommended by Cate, Declan peeled back the fabric once again to admire the familiar sheen of the wood. He'd missed it. Even now, his fingers itched to brush against the strings.

Each note he'd played for Maeve brought him immense joy. He'd played her a lover's lament, a tune that was slow yet intricate, a breaking of hearts. She'd grown wistful, closing her eyes until the song was over. When he'd finished, she'd smiled, touched a hand to his shoulder, and bid him goodnight.

Now he sat on the bed, allowing sheer relief to wash over him in waves. There was one person—a friend—who knew his true identity, and she treasured this knowledge.

As was his custom, he'd ducked inside Jess's house to start the record player. The faint notes of *Nessun dorma* perfumed the night with sound. He expected company any day now, the repeat invasion of an investigation. Until the dust settled, if it did, this concert would have to do.

"I suppose it's time we look for new digs," Declan said to the cat. With the stairs almost finished, there'd been no further mention of an eviction, yet Declan couldn't fathom staying. Watching another family clear out all memory of Jess, ridding the house of records and recipes, the stories that made it a cherished home, would be too much to watch. Declan was far from an expert on his own emotions, but heartache gripped him in this moment.

Lyncus chirruped from the countertop. With one paw, he batted at an item until it tumbled to the floor.

"What's this?" Declan reached for the brown paper package. It was small and rectangular. There was no tape, just an intricate system of folds and tucks.

Declan tore at the paper until he revealed a romance novel. On the cover, a man in a flowing white shirt held a woman arching backward from his grip. With one hand, he brushed at her cheek, the muscles of his jaw flexed. The couple's gazes were locked, his features determined, her mouth open in ecstasy at his simple caress.

"*An Inconvenient Flame,*" Declan read. He turned to Lyncus. "Guessing this isn't from you?"

Lyncus meowed, as though the answer were obvious.

"How did you know I needed a new story?" Declan spoke aloud as though his sister was still in the room. He flipped through the book. "Bet it's like *Wild Heat*. I know that's one of your fav—"

Mid-flip, something shiny fell from the pages and clattered on the floor. Declan bent to pick it up. From a blue ribbon dangled a key.

Declan twisted the object, considering its shape. The threads were familiar, somehow, however ordinary its design. "What do you suppose this goes to? Huh." He yawned, then tossed the key on the table. "I'll save that mystery for the morning."

Before he shut out the light, Declan paused to pick up Maeve's leaf. He twirled it between his thumb and forefinger, admiring the veins within the structure. "Of all those to call Astoria home," he said, musing. "If people only knew they had true royalty–the ancient kind–in their midst, Cate would have major front row competition at the studio." Declan shook his head and smiled. He set the leaf on the windowsill. "What if no one here is who they seem to be?"

"Well I'm certainly not," Lyncus said. While Declan gaped, the cat hopped onto the duvet, turned a tight circle, and went to sleep.

∾

THANK YOU!

Thanks so much for reading! If you enjoyed this book, please consider leaving me a review and I'll love you forever. Reviews help me find readers and I am grateful for all of you!

If there was something that tugged at your mind as you read, I'd love to hear from you at erinlarkmaples@gmail.com.

Deadly Nightshade, book two in the *Declan Rosewood Mysteries* will release in 2025. Join my newsletter to be the first to celebrate its release!

COMING EARLY 2025

Acknowledgments

Thank you to Jacque Hunter for digging out her Kindle while the lovely little Lyra was asleep. You are Joe's first and biggest fan.

Much thanks to Paula Lester, my editor-in-chief, who corrects, questions, pokes, prods, and otherwise looks for literary tweaks.

Appreciation to my family for their endless cheerleading of my art, no matter the form!

All my love to Bryan and Ava who subjected themselves to extra trips to Astoria to hike to random clifftop spots, drive circles around the historic neighborhoods, and listen to me bounce ideas off every wall in in town. You two are the best!

About the Author

Erin is a lover of fountain pens and the trail they leave behind. She's an award-winning author of cozy mysteries and fantasy whose work is praised for heart and snark as she breathes magic into the everyday.

A diehard gadabout and champagne fanatic, Erin is a firm believer in the tender and wild. This native Arizonan, when not behind a keyboard, can be found under the stars, howling at the moon.

Also by Erin Lark Maples

The Sheridan County Mysteries

The New Teacher

The Sled Dog

The Dead Swede

The Master Mechanic

The Banjo Player

The Declan Rosewood Mysteries

Bleeding Hearts

Deadly Nightshade (Spring 2025)

Four Crowns

Fallen

A Circle of Stars

Tiara Borealis (Fall 2024)

The Pie Maker's Apprentice